CHEROKEE TREASURE

Jeff Lovell

TotalRecall Publications, Inc.
1103 Middlecreek
Friendswood, Texas 77546
281-992-3131 281-482-5390 Fax
www.totalrecallpress.com

ISBN: 978-1-59095-234-4
UPC: 6-43977-42340-5

Library of Congress Control Number: 2018933798

Printed in the United States of America with simultaneous printings in Australia, Canada, and United Kingdom.

FIRST EDITION
1   2   3   4   5   6   7   8   9   10

This is a work of fiction. The characters, names, events, views, and subject matter of this book are either the author's imagination or are used fictitiously. Any similarity or resemblance to any real people, real situations or actual events is purely coincidental and not intended to portray any person, place, or event in a false, disparaging or negative light.

To the memory of my paternal
Grandmother, Susan Rowe Lovell, and
that of my father, Mr. Jack Lovell.
Grandmother Susan was a gentle, kind
woman who was the granddaughter of
a Choctaw woman and her husband.
She came to California from the Fort
Sill, Oklahoma, reservation to marry
my grandfather, Calvin Lovell.
Grandmother died before she could
see any of my achievements, my
family, my home, yet I knew her lovely
disposition, her kind nature, and her
loyalty. She was in my thoughts when
I worked with *Cherokee Treasure*.

Award Winning Author

is a native Chicagoan, with three degrees from the University of Illinois and an earned doctorate from Vanderbilt University.

Jeff taught high school writing and literature for thirty-three years and sponsored the school paper, Student Council and several other activities. He ran the drama program at two high schools, teaching and directing and designing sets, lighting and costumes. His specialty in his career focused on Shakespeare. Since he retired from education, Jeff has served as a theatre and film critic for a television station and appears frequently to review theatre and literature.

About the Book:

When I was a little boy, a great deal of television dealt with cowboys, and a great deal of that portrayed Indians as vicious killers. One movie had the lead character talking about the Oglala Sioux: "They're the throat cutters." But some of the most heroic and brilliant generals in our country's history were Native Americans: Crazy Horse, for example. Sitting Bull. Red Cloud, to name only a few. As a child, I was too young to have a sense of justice, I suppose, but I knew that it was wrong for the White Man to take the lands which were not theirs. It was wrong to slaughter the buffalo, as well, though the species seems to be making progress to repopulate now. Maybe I will succeed and give the land back to the Indians.

Prologue

The banker had made quite a bit of money in his career. He had a considerable amount of skill in investments and loan advisement, and had also made his clients a great deal of money over time. He had a beautiful wife, a lovely home, and two acceptable, though by no means exceptional, children.

He was not a happy man, however. His trophy wife, whom he learned after their marriage had married him for his wealth, was shopping her way into financial catastrophe for his bank accounts. She had a passion for fine clothes and expensive jewelry, and insisted on updating their furniture styles at a fairly frequent pace to grace their large and beautiful home. She joined the most exclusive health club in the area using the excuse that it catered to the express needs of women. Yeah, right, he sneered, but only to himself.

Despite all of his wife's lavish excess somehow, he had managed to stay in the black. Besides, her talents at sex made up for her lack of wisdom with finances, and she looked amazing in the expensive clothes when they attended social functions and events at their country club.

Then the crash hit and suddenly he found himself cash poor and deep in debt. He had obligations he had to meet, and in no way, could he round up that much money in such a short time. He recalled the cliché: desperate times called for desperate measures. Armed with his insider's knowledge of investments and having access to client accounts, he began raiding those that had remained inactive for a long period. He began rotating through accounts, being careful to take only what he considered to be inconsequential amounts at one time.

For some time, the banker had only been hiring employees whose intellectual curiosity would never extend to an investigation of his illegal activities. Within a short time, he began to regard his theft, while lucrative and virtually untraceable, as tedious and time consuming. He concluded that he needed a more workable solution to his problem.

One quiet afternoon at the bank when most of the employees had left for a long upcoming holiday weekend, he planned to stay and examine inactive accounts in more detail. And he hit pay dirt.

He found a couple whose names jarred his memory because they had died in a car crash and left a considerable fortune to their young daughter, an only child. But nothing ever materialized as to her whereabouts and the money remained untouched. The daughter, whose name was Janice, and would now be an adult, had never come forward to claim her inheritance. All efforts on the part of the bank to locate her had proved futile. He decided the bank must have made some mistakes when this account was set up and contact information was lost or misplaced.

The tragedy of this family offered him a unique and distinct opportunity for personal gain. This was definitely something worth spending time investigating. He began searching on his own and eventually discovered the daughter had been married and divorced, apparently unaware of her inheritance. He finally traced her to her current whereabouts and began to keep track of her. At the same time, he began raiding her account as unobtrusively as possible, keeping her location to himself. Soon he was able to pull level with his indebtedness, and he felt confident no one was onto his little scheme.

He even consulted his shady lawyer friend and convinced him to set up a phony will be designating him as beneficiary should she perish. He had to promise him a cut of the estate in the event of her death but considered it to be a small price for a huge pay-off.

Now he had to figure out how to arrange for the woman's death. In order to make his scheme work, he needed to be patient. As long as he could continue to withdraw her money undetected, he could manage that. Most important, he resolved not to make mistakes and to keep his eye on the prize. His trophy wife would be most pleased with his 'inheritance'.

*****

Now (War Chief) Roman Nose rode up on his white pony, his war bonnet trailing behind him, his face painted for battle. He called to the warriors not to fight singly, but to fight together as the soldiers did. He told them to form a long line on the open ground between the river and the bluffs. The warriors maneuvered their ponies into a line facing the warriors, with the Chief telling them to stand fast until he had emptied the soldiers' guns. Then he slapped his pony into a run and rode straight as an arrow toward one end of the line of soldiers. When he was close enough to see their faces clearly, he turned and rode fast along the length of the soldiers' line and they emptied their guns at him all along the way. At the end of the line he wheeled his white pony and rode back along the soldiers' front again…

--Brown, Dee. *Bury My Heart at Wounded Knee. New York: Holt, Rinehart and Winston, 1971.*

Prelude

Singing along with the Bon Jovi CD as they drove down the highway in their rented Jayco Precept RV on a beautiful summer night, the two couples could have been mistaken for rowdy teen-agers, their music blaring into their surroundings.

Paula and Daryl Mowen had picked up their good friends, Kay and Dave Himmelman for a well-deserved long week-end of camping and relaxing.

"Sweet wheels, Daryl," said an enthusiastic Dave, as he and Kay clambered into their home for the next few days.

"Told you, I wouldn't disappoint," replied Daryl.

Daryl was a thoracic surgeon whose work schedule almost drove him wacky. He often felt he spent more time in chests and abdomens than he did anything else and he was probably right. His wife, Paula, labored as a high powered matrimonial lawyer and while lucrative, it was an occupation involving much stress and way too many hours with argumentative spouses.

Kay and Dave were both urologists with stellar reputations whose services were in high demand all along the eastern seaboard. Vacation time was considered a luxury and needed to be scheduled well in advance.

Neither couple had children living at home any longer and both loved camping. Needless to say, the two couples were excited to get away on this four-day Labor Day weekend. By mutual agreement, neither couple brought along cell phones, computers and internet devices, or even the means of creating smoke signals. No, this weekend was going to be quiet, peaceful and totally without communication with the outside world.

"When I was a kid," said Daryl, "my grandparents lived in

Michigan City, Indiana, on the beach of Lake Michigan. They were good friends with some people named Martin, who owned a resort about a mile west of my grandparents."

"Really nice, huh?" smiled Dave.

"Surprisingly, no," said his friend. "It was really kind of a dump to look at. Oh, it was clean, pleasant, and restful. It had a unique advantage - Mr. Martin would never accept calls for one of his guests."

Dave thought for a second. Then, "Oh, I get it. That way no one could call them into the office, be yanked off vacation, nagged, etc."

"Exactly," said his friend with a grin. "Completely private, undisturbed. You had to book a room, five years in advance. Mostly, they were repeat customers."

They had a good laugh over this and Daryl gave Bunny, his rescue Irish Wolfhound, a pat on the rump. Bunny positioned herself in order to get her derrière rubbed. She was 120 pounds of pure sweetness and about as aggressive as, well, a bunny. Hence the name.

"Hey Daryl," teased Kay, "you do realize how funny that name is for that dog, don't you?"

"Hey, it fits her. Now don't you go making fun of my big, bad girl." laughed Daryl.

"You wouldn't believe all the comments we get," said Janice.

"Yes, I think I would," said Kay.

"Daryl even had to teach her to bark," giggled Janice.

"Oh, man, I would have given anything to see that lesson," hooted Dave.

Continuing south from Chattanooga, they eventually found the road to the deserted place where they would park the huge camper they had leased for the vacation. Kay, a genius at organization, had located a spot where they could camp, relax, and unwind with some fine food, good liquor, and nice weather.

Before they started back into the woods, they had stopped for gasoline and chatted with the local gas station attendant. Darryl produced the map they had been following, and showed him where they would be placing the camper for the weekend. He grew strangely quiet, and became a bit reluctant to talk. Still, he did give them good directions to their destination.

"That's old Indian territory," he said. "The Cherokee lived there long ago. Let me ask you something. Is your heart set on this place?"

Kay and Paula exchanged glances. Kay said, "Is there something wrong with the place?"

The attendant hedged and grew even more evasive. As they drove away, the two couples discussed his strange reaction to their vacation plans.

"What the hell did you make of that?" asked Dave.

"I don't know," admitted Darryl. "He sure got weird when we told him when we were going."

"He took me aside, just before we left," said Paula. "He said he was sorry if he upset us. He mentioned that the place has a reputation of being—well, haunted."

"Haunted!" exclaimed the other three.

"I don't know what to make of it," said Paula. "But he really appeared pretty rattled when he found out where we were going."

"Oh, for heaven's sake, Paula," said Dave, "it's probably just some local folklore promoted by some teen-angers who hang out in the woods and party."

"Come on," added Daryl, "we are highly educated adults and we certainly don't believe in ghosts or hauntings, do we?"

"Of course, you are right," said Paula. "I am being silly."

Kay piped up. "Hey, we have been anticipating this trip for a very long time. We aren't going to be scared off by some gas station guy we don't even know."

At that point the couples made a unilateral agreement not to be frightened, not to be superstitious, and to forget the gas station encounter.

"Let's get on with the party," said Dave.

With that announcement, Darryl had popped in some high-powered rock music, recorded when the group were high school kids, and in seconds the camper shook with a karaoke of vocalization.

They arrived at the property in the early afternoon, set up all their gear, arranged their folding chairs facing a beautiful view of the woods, and started the process of relaxing.

There was a stream flowing next to the campsite, which would be able to provide them with drinking water for their three-night stay in the woods. They had brought along a couple of portable water filters they had purchased online expressly for this trip. Both couples were excited for the opportunity to be out in the fresh air, hiking and grilling over an open fire.

They were looking forward to this weekend as a means for re-kindling the romantic aspect of their respective marriages, as well. The camper was large enough to ensure privacy for some much-needed intimacy. Sex tended to get pushed aside at times because of the high-powered jobs and the stress each couple had to combat in trying to make their marriages successful.

Darryl and Dave built a small campfire with some twigs and

bark, and pulled out some logs they'd brought along as back-up. The two couples sat, staring up at a beautiful full moon and agreed that life didn't get a whole lot better. Dave and Darryl told their wives about the sumptuous breakfast they'd planned for the morning.

"That sounds absolutely wonderful," said Kay, "but I am starving now. So, what have you guys got up your sleeve for tonight?"

"Just you wait here, little lady," drawled Daryl. Before long they were enjoying a dinner of thick filets, baked potatoes with all the trimmings, and grilled fresh asparagus, accompanied by a bottle of Pinot Noir.

"I trust that was satisfactory for you ladies," said Dave.

"Absolutely perfect," agreed the girls.

"And now, being fully satiated, it is time for the women to beat your butts in bridge," laughed Kay.

"You're on," said Daryl.

They proceeded to set up couples for their favorite card game. An exceptional scotch was brought out as an after-dinner drink, and while not drunk, they had a pleasant 'buzz', grateful they didn't have to drive any more that evening.

About ten-thirty they began saying their good nights, and were about to put out the lights and head into the camper. Abruptly, all the sounds of the night—the crickets and other creatures, the wind in the branches of the trees--were stilled. But in the sudden silence and to everyone's surprise, Bunny began barking and ran to hide behind Daryl.

Daryl, puzzled by her outburst, reached over and patted her. "It's all right, girl."

But Bunny continued for a couple of minutes, clearly furious or perhaps, frightened.

Bunny, who rarely barked unless given the command; "**speak**" in order to receive a treat, continued her cacophony, in obvious anger or to challenge something the rest of them couldn't see. Kay looked up the mountain and spied a small cave. The opening seemed to be glowing, as if someone had lit a campfire in the cave. They talked about it, but no one could remember seeing any cars on the road leading in.

"Who the heck would be in that cave?" asked Paula. "We are pretty much in the middle of nowhere—miles from any roads, villages."

Within moments, they received an answer.

Mesmerized, they watched a figure emerge from the cave. It scrabbled down the hillside until it reached the stream. The figure, which seemed to be hazy silver, leaped over the stream at the base of the hill and continued running down a path. It passed about twenty feet south of them and to their surprise, they thought that the figure was a middle-aged man dressed in striped pajamas, bedroom slippers and a bathrobe.

They could see what looked like a smile of triumph on the spectre's face. He looked like he was laughing at something, though what they couldn't imagine.

The phantasm ran down the path. Abruptly it stopped, flailing its arms and fell forward into a large oak tree.

"Ok, did you all see what I just saw?" asked Paula, her hands shaking a little.

Everyone nodded their head in agreement.

Darryl and Dave wasted no time in running over to see if they could render assistance, perhaps go into town for the local paramedics. The man had to have sustained a dreadful injury, ramming headlong into a solid old oak--

But there was no body. Nothing but a pile of leaves. No mark on the tree. No footprints. No blood. No trace whatever of a human body.

Darryl and Dave returned to their wives. Both husbands were used to blood and to death, as was Kay, but this didn't seem to be any sort of manifestation they had ever seen.

They sat waiting but nothing else happened. The light was out in the cave, and a quiet, peaceful stillness settled over the little valley where they were camped.

"Maybe we had a little too much to drink," suggested Kay.

They were all baffled, and frankly frightened by something so utterly out of their experience, though unwilling to admit as much out loud. Instead they decided to call it a night and retired to their rooms in the camper. The couples had been anticipating this time of night, but the sexual encounters they'd discussed and frankly looked forward to eluded them.

After a troubled night's sleep, both couples rose early and met over steaming cups of coffee and a campfire built to remove the chill from the early morning air. They tried to make sense of the events of the previous night. "Did we really see that—that—whatever it was?" asked the women.

Their husbands assured them that they had. They faced a decision about whether they should go home.

"Well, I have to admit I am a little freaked out about this," admitted Kay, "but I don't feel threatened with all of you here with me. I vote we stay."

Paula added, "I agree. We have had this week-end, in the works for a long time, and we had a great evening together last night. Let's just forget about it and go on with our plans.

The guys nodded and Dave said, "Well, if you girls are ok with staying, we will continue with our plans. We certainly have a plentiful supply of food and libations."

The breakfast that had been promised the day before was prepared and disappeared with little difficulty. The girls offered to be the cleanup crew since the men had prepared the meal.

"Everyone ready for that five-mile hike, we planned on taking?" asked Paula a short time later.

They all groaned but agreed to the exercise regimen. Once they began their walk, all were glad they didn't give in to their lazy impulses. They witnessed all kinds of wildlife and beautiful scenery.

Upon their return, Darryl, who fancied himself an expert grill master, started the ribs in the early afternoon over a low, slow fire. By seven o'clock, the food was ready expertly grilled ribs, terrific baked potato, a great chef's salad, all set off by a splendid California Petit Syrah. A triple chocolate cheesecake purchased at the Cheesecake Factory rounded out the outstanding meal.

The two couples moved chairs over by the campfire and sat enjoying a nice B and B liqueur, with its' sweet finish and exquisite nose.

"Now that was some meal," announced Kay. "I will say, we have to give you guys high marks this trip for your culinary skills. So glad we decided to stay. This was one of those perfect days you always remember."

"For sure," agreed Paula. "In fact, I may just cede all the cooking in the household over to you, Daryl."

But then, Bunny again began to bark, furious and loud. The two women screamed. The Light was on again in the cave, and the same figure raced down the hillside. Again, the leap. The sneer. The run. The trip on the root.

Then, all was quiet.

A frantic effort ensued and within the hour the couples had packed the huge camper, and driven out of the valley. This time, they were deeply shaken by finding themselves in a situation their analytic, rational and highly trained minds could not explain. They parked the camper and spent a couple nights in a resort hotel far from the campsite.

On the way home, they stopped in to see the police to report what had happened. The cop came in to takes their statements.

He smiled and nodded his head as he wrote down the information. He explained, "I have to tell you, this is not the first time I have heard this very same story. No, I'll write up the report. I do believe you, and I'm sure you were scared. I don't blame you. What I'm going to tell you next is what's going to be hard to believe."

"Why didn't we find a body?" asked Darryl.

"Yeah," said Dave. "The guy hit the tree and collapsed."

"Well," said Jim. "If you'd dig around there, you'd probably find some fossilized bits."

"Fossilized?" said Kay and Janice at the same moment.

"Well, yeah," said Jim. "His body has been there for more than 500 years."

He then reached into a folder and pulled out a poster which, he said, had been posted all over their area. When they saw the face of the missing man the poster detailed, Dave said, "What the—that is the same guy we saw running in the woods."

They decided their next camping trip would be planned more carefully and definitely would avoid those woods.

CHAPTER ONE

The Atlantic Ocean,
off the coast of Ocracoke,
North Carolina

Janice O'Neill pulled out of her hometown of Washington, North Carolina, heading for the Big City of Raleigh and from there to Chapel Hill. Nothing stood in her way now, she told herself. But even within that in mind, the tears still wouldn't stop. The scene with her husband had been as bitter, rancorous and nasty as a walk-through perdition.

He'd confronted her on a few occasions, asking if there was another man. She lied on those occasions, claiming that the rumors and gossip were idiotic.

But then, yesterday, he asked her to come out in the car with him. They drove in pregnant silence to the Pamlico Sound.

Once they'd parked, he said, "Okay. I can't take the lying and the hiding, the whole life of prevarication."

He'd had to define prevarication, but she denied the charges of adultery with all the power of lying that she could muster. It went on for a few moments, but then he pulled out The Envelop.

Pictures. Copies of receipts. Motel bills. He even had a cassette tape that his investigator had made…

"You hired an investigator?" she asked, in unbelief. He gave a thin smile, and nodded.

"Okay," he said. "I've got you. It's over, Janice."

"Over?" she mumbled.

"Our so-called marriage, of course," he snarled. "I want you out of the house, as soon as possible. Take your clothes, your possessions, but leave the pictures, the records, the …"

"I get the picture," she managed.

"I'll not pay any alimony if you oppose the divorce," he said. "I'm going to try for an annulment, given that you've never really been married to me, and I'll fight you as vigorously as God gives me strength."

"I see," she stammered.

"Now," he said. "I'm going to take the girls out of town for the night, and you can have your possessions."

Janice, stunned, didn't have anything to say. They drove back to the house in silence, and she waited in the garage while her husband packed up some clothes for their daughters and left, leaving her alone, numb and nauseated.

When he was gone, taking their daughters out of her life, she went in and began to pack, tears trickling down her cheeks. She didn't sleep much that night.

Janice, a full-blooded Cherokee, had grown up to be a beautiful woman. She was tall with a regal posture, and shiny black hair which she wore long and flowing. People who saw her would find themselves thinking of pictures of Indian women from the early days of photography. Her intellect, while profound, remained undisciplined and unfocused. After dropping out of college, she'd done little to hone her mental skills.

It wouldn't take too long to straighten out the mess she'd made in marrying that schoolteacher Patrick O'Neill, she figured as she drove. Yeah. Her life was about to change in a radical way. Soon, she would be married to a rich real estate tycoon, and she'd be financially secure, enjoying a new place in society, and being happy for a change.

She'd called Steve, the real estate guy she'd been sleeping with when she could sneak away from Patrick and the two girls. She left a message on his phone machine, and intended to meet Steve in the Student Union of the University of North Carolina in Chapel Hill.

She'd had a dashing affair with him for a few months now, and it was time to move the relationship along. First, she'd divorce Patrick, and almost immediately marry Steve. She'd tried again to call her soon-to-be husband at a drug store pay phone as she left the outskirts of Washington, but he didn't answer his phone. In another twenty years or so, she'd be able to call him on a cell phone, but that technology was unknown to her as she drove. Now, she'd wait until she arrived at the college. He'd probably be there already, she giggled to herself.

She wriggled a little in anticipation of being with Steve that night. She and Patrick had lost all interest in intimacy with one another. He'd never seemed to be able to offer her the satisfaction to which she felt entitled, but that would change now.

Janice, with her simplistic reasoning, figured that both she and Steve could get divorced quickly, and marry right after that.

She blew her nose, wiped the tears and tried to pull herself together. Come on, she thought. She liked the idea of being married to Steve. He had a lot of money from his real estate business on the coast, in communities up and down the Eastern Sea Board. He'd be able to step seamlessly into whatever community they'd move into, naturally. He was a top-notch property mover. He'd told her plenty of stories about how he'd screwed over people, chuckling as he related the tales. She'd watched him take some of those Washington, North Carolina rubes down the garden path in some dog of a house, making terrific profits by making promises he couldn't fulfill, and never would fulfill.

He'd also snicker on occasion when he'd tell her about the preposterous deals—well, swindles would be the better word--he'd finished. She loved the stories, thinking about how great it was going to be once she left her husband.

Janice felt the niggling worry about what he did and how he made a living. She had the feeling that this wasn't legal. In fact, she felt sure that he could go to jail. Then what?

No, she said to herself. She wasn't going to dwell on that. She couldn't consider such a thing. She forced the feeling down and tried to focus elsewhere.

Janice knew that men were attracted to her beauty. She'd never acted on that attraction when she first married Pat. She was true to her vows, at least for a few years.

The best part—at least, one of the best—was being free at last of money worries: no more humiliating financial problems, like scrimping, walking along the road to find soda pop bottles to return for deposit. While married to Patrick she found herself saving pennies, looking between the cushions of the crummy living room couch for coins that had fallen out of pockets. Patrick O'Neill, a career teacher, made a terrible salary in a state where the taxpayers have always paid their teachers low wages.

For a moment, she again allowed herself to ponder her marriage to Pat. They'd been married more than ten years, producing two children. They were in fourth and third grade and never did well despite Patrick working with them night after night. Patrick, in a cynical mood, had told her that the only reason they learned was so that he'd leave them alone. Yeah. That was probably it, all right.

She swallowed hard not to feel guilt about leaving the girls, despite their miserable attitudes, laziness, and absolute disinterest in doing anything worthwhile. After all, they had rejected her, rejected everything she'd tried, like reading to them, helping with arithmetic and trying to inspire them to do well. They would sit for hours in front of the TV, or behind locked bedroom doors, not playing outside, and they had limited friendships with the other kids in the neighborhood.

But they were still her daughters and deep down she did love them. She struggled not to be ashamed of herself. Janice thought about how she and Patrick would cry. They would plead and punish. They would cajole and bribe, all to no avail. The girls would scream back at them, telling her that they hated her, hated North Carolina, refusing even to try to do well.

Still, if there was any part of leaving the marriage that truly bothered her, it was leaving the girls. She didn't like admitting defeat, but she knew that was what happened. The girls had beaten her down.

On the other hand, now that she thought about it, this was working out pretty well. She tried telling herself that she wouldn't have to deal with her daughters any more. She'd left them with Patrick, and soon she'd get a couple of new kids with Steve. Well, say after a few years. And immediately she knew she was lying to herself as a tear rolled down her cheek.

Her engine gave a little chug of protest. She glanced at the gas gauge and realized that she'd forgotten to fill up the crummy wreck. She saw a gas station up ahead and pulled in. She grinned to herself, thinking of how she'd grabbed the food money for the month before leaving. Patrick didn't realize he was subsidizing her getaway.

She told the attendant to fill it up, and the rusty heap belched down eight bucks worth. She handed him the old, beat-up Standard Oil credit card, and he was back in a few moments. She noticed that the name tag on his shirt identified him as Gus.

"Sorry, Ma'am," he said. "This card has been cancelled."

"What?" she gasped. He nodded. "But I just used it last week."

"I can't help that," he said. "Meanwhile, you owe me eight bucks."

She gave him another charge card. Then another. In a matter of moments, she saw the truth: Patrick had cancelled all her credit cards, probably yesterday before he threw her out.

She dug out eight dollars—a five and three singles-- and handed it over. He now relaxed a bit, and made a little joke that was lost on her. She stood in a little shock. She hadn't thought that she was going to have to go into her cash reserves for a few days anyway.

"Oh, well," said the attendant. Now Janice realized that he found her attractive. With an eye toward pleasing her husband-to-be, she'd put on a skirt shorter than what she usually wore, showing off her long lovely legs. She also wore a somewhat revealing blouse and her best high heels. She'd spent considerable time on her hair and makeup as well. She decided to see if she could exploit the attraction he felt.

"Sir, I'm going to be looking for a job," she said. "I'm new in town. Need any help?"

"I'm afraid not today," he said. Then he paused and gave her an up and down look, taking in the revealing blouse, the too-short skirt, and the brassy high heels. He cleared his throat. "You know, though, I might by the end of the week, say Saturday."

"I'll keep that in mind," she said. "Will you remember me?" He smiled and nodded his head. She was pretty sure he'd remember her.

Two minutes later she was back on the road. She wouldn't need it, but it's always good to cover your bases, she told herself. Smiling, she settled in for the drive to Chapel Hill, now only a few minutes away.

*****

The white man has taken our country, killed all of our game; was not satisfied with that, but killed our wives and children. Now no peace. We want to go and meet our families in the spirit land. We loved the whites until we found out they had lied to us, and robbed us of what we had…

Chief Leg-in-the-Water, quoted in *Bury My Heart at Wounded Knee.*

--by Dee Brown. Holt, Rinehart and Winston, 1971, p. 94.

CHAPTER TWO

Rather to her surprise, Janice found a parking space in a campus lot in front of the Hume Undergraduate Library. Then she thought, Oh sure. It's summer. Not as crowded as it will be in a couple of months.

She locked up her car, and walked west a little bit, making her way to the Graham Student Union. She went in the front door and found a washroom to repair her hair and make-up. Returning to the main reception area, she found an empty chair where she could sit and wait for the man who would soon become her new husband.

But then, an hour passed. Another. Then another.

Several students walked by, and more than a few looked at her. She didn't understand why they paid her any attention whatever. Then she realized. The students were, in general, well dressed, and she was wearing a sluttish short skirt and a revealing tee shirt. A man sat down next to her and greeted her.

"You've been sitting here for quite a while," he said.

"I guess so," she shrugged, trying not to encourage him, tugging self-consciously at the hem of her tiny skirt.

"Are you waiting for someone?" he asked.

"Excuse me, sir," she said. "I don't know you, and I'm sure we've never met. I'd rather not discuss my business with you if you don't mind."

"Of course, of course," he said. "I'm a bit different than the other people here. I'm campus security." He showed her a badge.

"Oh. I see. Okay," she said, thinking, I guess I'm a bit more touchy today than I realized. She offered a little apology for being rude and brusque. She explained, "I'm supposed to meet my fiancé, I mean, in the Union. We said we'd meet near the front door at ten o'clock and then go to have lunch. Now it's almost one o'clock, and he hasn't shown up. I'm a little worried."

"Do you have a phone number?" he asked. "For your friend, I mean?"

"Well, yes…" she began.

"Okay," he said. "How about coming to my office? I think you might be a bit more comfortable there."

Janice hesitated. Then, she thought, here's someone trying to be nice. Might as well. "Thank you," she said, and took his hand. She allowed him to help her up.

"My name is Ron Whiteside," smiled the man, handing her a business card. "I'm the head of campus security. I told my guys I'd handle this myself, and I have to tell you that some of them were a bit envious."

Janice managed to smile, but she was feeling a little weak with worry. What if Steve had gotten in an accident? Could he be hurt? Maybe some other sort of emergency? She tried to shrug away her misgivings. Her stomach felt more than a little queasy with nervousness as she tried to get hold of herself.

Whiteside gave her a chair and pulled the phone around to her. "Dial 9 first," he said. Janice tapped the button, and then listened for a dial tone. She typed in Steve's number.

Two minutes later, she hung up the phone.

"He's not answering his phone," she said.

"Not a big surprise," said Whiteside, with a shrug of his shoulders. "If he's on his way to meet you, he couldn't answer his phone, right?"

Janice thought, and then agreed. She picked up the phone

again, and tapped the 9 to get a dial tone. Now she tried Steve's real estate office. His secretary answered on the third ring.

"Lucille, this is Janice," she said. "Is Steve there?"

A silence descended on the line. "Lucille?" she asked into the receiver.

"Just a minute," said Lucille, and the line went dead. Clearly Lucille had put her on hold.

Even now she didn't suspect the truth.

"What's happening?" asked Whiteside.

"I don't know," said Janice. "They usually put me right in."

"Yeah," he said. Two minutes went by.

"Mrs.—er—O'Neill?" said a male voice at last.

"Yes, this is Janice O'Neill," she said.

"Mrs. O'Neill, I'm sorry to be the one telling you this," said the man. "My name is Ted Thomas. I'm an attorney. I'm the security officer for this firm."

She thought, A real estate company has a security officer? She said, "Uh-huh?"

"The Office here has retained me to deal with the situation," he replied.

"Situation?" she asked.

"Mr. Bragg isn't here, nor is he with our company anymore," said the man. "He was relieved of his duties over a week ago. Some of the people here in the office said he's skipped town, if you know what I mean."

"Skipped town?" gasped Janice. Whiteside's eyebrows went up. Then he nodded, almost as if he'd anticipated this outcome.

"Yes," said the man. "Several of them believe that he has gone to the west coast."

"But…" she said.

"I'm sorry, Mrs. O'Neill," said Thomas. "I hope you didn't buy a house from him."

"But why?" she asked.

"He's been selling homes here in town and along the coast without a real estate license for a couple of months," Thomas told her. "He had forged a license, and we didn't realize it. We're trying to clean up the mess he left us now."

"A mess," she said.

"Oh yeah," said the detective. "He would offer the buyers astounding deals on homes they, under most circumstances, couldn't have afforded."

"And he would then steal the down payments and the earnest money," mumbled Janice.

"Exactly," said Mr. Thomas. "So, if you are one of his victims, why, we can put you on the list and try to help out…"

"No, thank you," said Janice. "I'm a different sort of victim, I think."

*****

In the Moon When the Snow Drifts into the Tepees (January 1870) an ugly rumor came from the country of the Blackfeet. Somewhere on the Marias River in Montana, soldiers had surrounded a camp of Piegan Blackfeet and slain them like rabbits trapped in a hole…The Army tried to keep the massacre secret, announcing only that Major Eugene M. Baker had led a cavalry command out of Fort Ellis, Montana, to punish a band of Blackfeet horse thieves…Of the 219 Piegans in the camp, only 46 escaped to tell the story: 33 men, 90 women and 50 children were shot to death as they ran from their lodges.

--By Brown, Dee. *Bury My Heart at Wounded Knee*. p. 178.

Chapter Three

Janice hung up the phone and turned to the man who had befriended her.

"Now what do I do?" she stammered. Whiteside asked her a few questions.

Janice didn't hear much, and so she couldn't respond too well. He gave her a glass of water, and then offered her a peppermint from a candy jar on his desk.

"Do you have a place to stay?" asked Whiteside.

"Well, no," she managed. "I have all my clothes in the car. I have most of my personal belongings, too. Nothing of much value, though."

"You mean you came over here without a place to stay?"

"I thought my—er—friend had an apartment here, I mean, near the University," she said. "I planned to move in with him for a little while, whatever time it took."

"Uh, huh," said Whiteside. "Would you like for me to arrange a room for you for a couple of nights?"

"But—where?" asked Janice.

"We could put you up here at the Carolina Inn," said Whiteside. "We have some very nice rooms, and since it's summer, not too many people are here in the hotel. Tomorrow you could apply for a job here, that is, at the University, if you wanted. I know they could use some help this week."

"Doing what?" she asked. Her brain still wasn't really working too well.

Whiteside replied. "Oh, general housekeeping, cleaning, getting the place ready for the students. Want me to take you to the employment office?"

Janice agreed and squeaked out a 'thank you', but she was numb, now, and she let him lead her from place to place. She agreed that she could start in the morning working as a maid in the hotel rooms.

Janice worked on her feet pretty well, usually, but the day had been too much for her. She certainly didn't feel she could go back to her husband. He'd thrown her out. But now what?

Whiteside smiled. "Look at it this way," he said. "It's a good temp job."

"I guess so," she said. He showed her where to park her car, retrieved a cart to help her move her stuff into the room, and made sure she was comfortable. At last she was settled in the room. Whiteside smiled.

"Hungry?" he asked.

She looked up. She hadn't thought about it.

"Goodness," she said. "Yes. I'm starving. Is there a fast food place…?"

"To hell with the fast food," he said. "Why don't you let me take you a little bit nicer place?"

Numbly, she nodded. "Okay," she said.

"Great. Take a shower, put on a dress, and we'll go to a little place I know. I've got some things to close up, tonight. I'll pick you up about 6:30 when you've rested a little bit."

He turned to go. "Mr. Whiteside," Janice mumbled. He opened the door, and turned to look at her.

"Yeah?" he grinned.

"You've been wonderful to me," said Janice, still numb. Then she flew across the room to his arms.

She hadn't thought about such a thing. She couldn't stop

crying now. He returned the embrace and smiled at her. "I get paid to help people out," he responded.

*****

"I am but one man. I am the voice of my people…My skin is red; my heart is a white man's heart: but I am a Modoc. I am not afraid to die. When I die my enemies will be under me. Your soldiers began on me when I was asleep in Lost River. They drove us to these rocks, like a wounded deer…

--Kintpuash (Captain Jack) of the Modocs. Dee Brown, 1971. P. 219.

CHAPTER FOUR

Whiteside came to her room in the Carolina Inn and found her wearing a pretty sundress and heels. She had done her hair up, put on fresh makeup and her eyes were brighter. The outfit was far less provocative than her travel outfit. Indeed, she looked very nice.

"Yeow," he said.

"Yeow?" she smiled.

"You look terrific," he said. She felt tears starting at the sweet compliment and his attention.

"Thank you," she said, near to crying at the flattering remark. The kind words were a much-needed compliment. His grin made her smile, and she managed to put away the tears. I can't cry every time I'm with this man, she thought.

He drove her to a place called Smitty's, a pleasant restaurant outside of town. The management knew him, and gave him a choice table.

Dinner featured a nice bottle of wine, candlelight, soft music, and delicious Carolina seafood, some of the best in the world. As the meal ended, she asked him about why he was being so kind to her.

"Do you just want to get me into bed?" she asked, her face mischievous.

"I can't deny that it would be stupendous," he said. "But no, this is just to get to know you. I'm a long way from attempting seduction."

"You are?" she asked, with a smile.

"I don't think even I could be so churlish as to take

advantage of you tonight," he said. "Maybe in a few more dates." Janice chuckled. "No, the last thing you need is a romantic involvement."

"I start my training for the maid job in the morning," she said. He nodded.

"Yeah," he said. "Look, I don't want to get personal, but didn't you say you went to college for a while?"

She shrugged. "For two years. It was a local community college. I got an Associate's degree. Then I met my husband. I decided that since he had a degree, I didn't need one. I dropped out."

He grimaced. "So, how'd you do?"

"You mean with grades?" she asked. He nodded. "I did well," she said. "Almost all A's."

His mouth dropped open. "Said what?" She'd always done very well in school. Ron asked, "And you didn't continue?"

"I dropped out and got married to my husband about six months later. We got along okay at first."

"I can imagine," he said, and she grinned at the compliment.

"Thank you. But after a while, we had almost nothing in common. My husband had a master's degree, he taught at a high school, and taught Shakespeare, Dickens, Steinbeck—all that. I tried to read what he worked with, but I couldn't do it. I just couldn't understand the metaphors in which the great authors wrote. I had two children, both girls, and didn't get how to raise them. Frankly, I was a terrible mother. I seem to lack completely the ability to raise children." She told him a little about her daughters and her humiliating failure with them.

"Do you feel that way now?" he asked. "I mean, that you'd

be a terrible mother?"

"Well," she shrugged, "I guess I have to go with the evidence."

"Back to college," he said. She lifted an eyebrow in question. "You don't have to make a decision. But employees do get a break on tuition, you know. Why don't you think about taking some course work while you work here?"

Janice was surprised. She said she'd consider it, but it did sound pretty good. After all, the University of North Carolina at Chapel Hill had a fine academic reputation. Indeed, it had a stellar reputation in both academic and athletic areas. She'd regretted many times that she hadn't finished a degree. Now with the way things were turning out perhaps she should consider college again.

*****

"My heart is as stone; there is no spot in it. I have taken the white man by the hand, thinking him to be a friend, but he is not a friend; government has deceived us; Washington is rotten."

--Chief Kicking Bird of the Kiowas, quoted in *Bury My Heart at Wounded Knee*. p. 262

CHAPTER FIVE

The next morning, Janice ate a light breakfast at the cafeteria in the Union. Her money was okay for the moment but she knew she couldn't be profligate. She trudged over to the campus employment office, and began going through the usual rigmarole of acquiring a uniform, training, and so on. Janice hadn't really had a legitimate job for some years.

As she worked, Janice thought about her life. She decided that a part time supplement to her maid's salary would not be a bad idea. When she finished work that afternoon, she went back to her room and dressed in one of her seductive outfits. She drove to the gas station she'd traded with on her way into town.

The owner stared at her for a few moments, not remembering her from her previous visit at first. Then he recalled. "Can you start tonight?" he asked.

"Sure," she said. "I know how to pump gas, anyway."

He grunted. "Okay," he said. "I have a room in back if you want to change. Probably that skirt and heels wouldn't work too well here."

Janice pulled her suitcase out of her car trunk and extracted a tee shirt and a pair of jeans. She changed in the women's washroom into the work outfit and put on some jogging shoes.

"Okay," said the owner, whose name was Gus Triandos. "How about cleaning up the place to start out with?"

Janice nodded with a smile. One thing she knew how to do was to clean. She was working a few moments later as a customer pulled up to the pumps. "Come on," said the owner. "I'll show you what to do."

"Sure," she said.

The customer chose a fill-up and paid with a credit card, so she learned to use the machine to transmit the card information. The owner offered her the back room of the station as a place to stay, and gave her a key to the room. The washrooms were pretty disgusting, but she cleaned them till they were more than habitable. The owner had a couple of showers in the men's room that were intended for truckers. The showers would serve her well.

So, the back room of a service station began to evolve into living quarters for Janice. The owner was delighted at the way the washrooms had cleaned up, and bought her paint and supplies to make them attractive to customers.

The owner closed the service station at 7:00 p. m. and Janice went back to her room at the Carolina Inn. Before she went up to her room, she settled her bill and arranged to move out in the morning, feeling lucky to have secured a free room at the garage.

*****

Of the 3,700,000-buffalo destroyed from 1872 through 1874, only 150,000 were killed by Indians…The free Kwahadis wanted no part of a civilization that advanced by exterminating useful animals.

--Brown, D.. *Bury My Heart at Wounded Knee*, 1971. p. 262.

CHAPTER SIX

She went to work the next morning at the gas station and pumped gas from 7:00 a. m. until 9:00 a. m., when the owner relieved her. Then, she changed clothes into her maid's outfit and cleaned rooms at the union until after lunch. As she was about to finish, her new boss came in to do an inspection.

Janice was a little nervous, but he smiled and pronounced her work satisfactory. At 3:30 that afternoon she changed and drove back to the gas station. Between customers she worked in the back room setting up her living quarters.

At 7:00 p. m., the gas station owner closed up the service station. Janice went into the washrooms and cleaned, painted and then decorated them until about eleven, when she collapsed on the bed.

At 7:00 the next morning, she opened the station and began the routine of the day again. Over the next several days, Janice found that she enjoyed working at the gas station. After a few weeks, the owner began teaching her how to do some of the less difficult mechanical jobs, such as changing oil for customers, using the hydraulic lifts, rotating and repairing tires, and other things.

Her customers, in particular the men, liked the novelty of a female grease monkey. Indeed, she rather surprised herself as she demonstrated an aptitude for the work. The owner told people that he was surprised at how readily she would learn to perform the difficult mechanical work.

Janice, for her part, saw her jobs as a matter of working hard to establish a life for herself. In her diligence, she had little time to herself, which was good, she thought. She felt that the discipline of the hard work was a facet that had been missing in her life. The highlight of each week, the moment she pointed toward, was a standing date with her friend Ron, the Head of Security from the University.

Several weeks later and even after many dates, Janice didn't suggest intimacy with her new friend. As she thought about it, she'd been casual about who she slept with for several years. She'd had several unsatisfactory affairs, and she had come to regard the extramarital sex as her way of getting back at the world.

She thought for a few moments about that. AIDS had been receiving a great deal of publicity and she really hadn't paid too much attention to the stories she'd read. None of the men she'd met could possibly be infected, could they? Certainly not this man Ron Whiteside, who'd been so good to her at a time she desperately needed help. Surely not.

*****

Ron took her to see a very funny movie one night, an encore showing of Mel Brooks' Blazing Saddles. She all but staggered with laughter even as they left the theatre. Then he surprised her by taking her to a beautiful seafood restaurant for crabcakes, good martinis and a bottle of a delicious Gewurztraminer, icy cold with a delicate bouquet that complemented the outstanding fish and elegant presentation.

"Ron," she smiled. "I don't expect this from you. I'm certainly not complaining…"

"I hope not," he laughed. "I'm just a poor cop."

"What I mean is, you know--" she began and faltered. He asked the question.

"Am I up to something?" he smiled.

"Well, yes," she said.

"I am, yes," Ron told her, looking her straight in the eye.

"This is really bad, isn't it?"

He hesitated. "I don't know," he said. "Here it is." Now he hesitated. She felt a little ill.

After a few moments, she faltered, "Don't leave me hanging. You're scaring me."

He looked at her. "I've been struggling for a few days trying to figure out how to say this right. I've been offered a job the University of Washington. It's a faculty job, so I'll do some teaching and work with students. I'll finally be able to use my Ph. D."

She sat staring, thunderstruck. She couldn't speak for fear of sobbing with the pain. "Oh," she said, trying not to disappoint him.

"Why are you looking so sad?" he asked.

"What do you think?" she lashed out, and now she couldn't hold the tears back. "My best friend," she wailed. "Really, other than Gus at the station, you're my only friend. You're the only person who helped me out when I showed up here broke and all alone. And now you're leaving?"

"I didn't know you'd feel this strongly," he said.

"Of course, I feel this strongly," she replied.

"Well, then," he said, "How about coming with me?"

Janice's mouth dropped open. "What?" she choked, though it took a few moments.

"Yeah," he said. "I know that this is pretty sudden, and we've only known each other a little while. I also know that you've been trying to build a new life here. You've been working hard to set up an independent life, and taking classes toward a degree and a career for yourself."

"I don't see…" she began.

"If I'm on the staff at Washington," he smiled, "you could get free tuition as my wife."

But she didn't love him. Respect him, value his friendship, enjoy his company, yes, but she didn't want to marry if love wasn't present. She tried not to hurt him.

"I'm just starting to get my life going," she explained. "I've got a couple of good jobs, and I'm learning so much at the gas station. I don't want to back away from what I'm doing."

She felt awful as he drove her home. Somehow, she knew he wasn't going to be part of her life ever again.

A few days later, they still hadn't spoken again. A package arrived, containing a good-bye note from her friend Ron, expressing sadness that things hadn't worked out. Several items—a scarf, a jacket, and a couple of little knick-knacks—were packed in the box.

She had a good cry for quite a while that evening. She thanked God that their relationship had not gone further. If they had, she knew that she would never have been able to make a clean break. After a few days, she felt somewhat better. She didn't love him, and she knew it.

Time went by so quickly that she was amazed as she thought about it. By the middle of autumn, she'd become skilled at her jobs. The owner of the gas station showed her how to do repairs that were a bit more sophisticated, and she soon became proficient at them.

At first, the tasks seemed complicated and made little sense. However, routine things like changing oil and tuning up engines became jobs she could accomplish without supervision. The customers were a little wary at first at the idea of a beautiful woman doing mechanical work, but when they saw her intense effort to do a good job, they began to request that she do the work on their cars. The owner was delighted to cede the work to her.

*****

(By 1875) The great leaders were gone; the mighty power of the Kiowas and Comanches was broken; the buffalo they had tried to save had vanished. It had all happened in less than ten years.

--Brown, Dee. *Bury My Heart at Wounded Knee*, p. 271.

CHAPTER SEVEN

One day as she was working at the station, she heard a car chug into the parking lot and turned to see a huge Cadillac pull up to a self-serve pump. Janice put down her socket wrench and walked to the car.

"Sir," she said to the owner.

"Yeah?" he snarled.

"Uh—" she said, stunned at the rude tone. "Your car needs a very simple repair. You have a faulty gas filter. I could fix it for you in a few moments. Or, you can keep driving and pray that you make it another block or so. Up to you."

His response was profane and sneering, and his rudeness made her draw back in surprise. "Okay," she said. "I only wanted to be helpful. That'll be 20 dollars for the fill-up." He took a twenty-dollar bill, wadded it up into a green spitball and threw it at her face. Janice caught the money, shrugged, said 'Thank you' with as much sincerity as she could muster and walked back to the car she was working on.

She heard the car start up and drive away. The chugging had gotten worse. A few moments later, she heard car horns honking.

She had to smile as she turned to look. The car had died in the middle of the street.

The car sat, sullenly refusing to start. Janice continued her work on the small compact she'd been tuning up.

The boss rose from behind his desk. "What just happened?" he asked. Janice filled him in. "Okay," he said. The man climbed out of his Caddy and walked over to the service bay where Janice was working.

"Yes?" said Gus, stepping in.

"I want her to fix my car," said the man, belligerence in every fiber.

"I'm sorry," said the owner. "Our services are not available. Good day."

Janice turned back to her work, her heart in her throat. The man shoved the owner aside and advanced on her. Now, she smelled the liquor on his breath.

"Damn it!" yelled the man, his mouth a foot from her ear. Now he grabbed her shoulder and pulled her around to face him. "I said I want— "

Janice grabbed a deep socket from her tools and wrapped her fingers around it. She pivoted and slammed her fist into the man's throat. It was like she hit him with a lead pipe.

The customer gasped, choked and tried to speak. He staggered backward and sat down hard on the driveway. The owner and the other mechanic from the next service bay pinioned his arms, but he was still so stunned he couldn't speak, just barely able to utter croaking profanity.

Janice, enraged, grabbed a huge box wrench from her toolbox and advanced on him.

"No, Janice," said the owner, stepping in front of her. "He's done. I called 911. The cops are on the way."

Within two minutes a squad car arrived and the police handcuffed the man. They shoved him into the back seat. The owner told one of the policemen what had happened.

Janice's rage had begun to fade and she felt the emotion of the incident.

The other policemen took her arm in a gentle, kind grasp and drew her into the office. She told him her version of the events.

The cop shook his head. "What a thug," he said, contempt in his voice. "We'll take him in."

"If he'd apologized for his behavior," she said, "instead of being so belligerent, I could have fixed his car in a moment."

The policeman nodded. "Don't worry. He won't be back. I think he'll enjoy his next several meals at the expense of the city jail."

He started to leave and then turned back. "Between you and me?" he asked. She turned to look at him. "Good job. He deserved it." He gave her a card and insisted that she let him know if she saw him again.

The incident had scared Janice, who had to struggle to hold back the tears that threatened to force their way down her cheek. "Thank you," she said. "I appreciate your help."

Gus came into the office as the policeman left. "You want to take the rest of the day off?" he asked.

She considered. "No, I don't think so, I don't have any place to go. I'd just sit around the back room and stew about this."

"I doubt that you'd just sit around," he said, smiling at her with approval. "You were pretty brave."

"I took a few self-defense classes about five years ago. It's the first time I've ever needed to use what I learned."

He held up the socket wrench. "Want to finish that Volkswagen?"

"Sure," she said. "It won't take long."

*****

We want no white men here. The Black Hills belongs to me. If the whites try to take them, I will fight.

--Chief Sitting Bull, quoted in *Bury My heart at Wounded Knee*, p. 273.

CHAPTER EIGHT

Janice finished work at about 7:15. Gus told her to get cleaned up and relax for the evening. A quick shower in the back room and a change into some clean clothes made her feel much better.

She thought about what the owner had told her had happened when he went to press charges at the Police Station. Gus had said to the drunken thug, "She's reliable and a fine mechanic. People ask for her to work on their cars all the time.

"You aren't welcome at my shop again," Gus continued. "Not only that, I've got your address and I know now where you live. If you ever come near her again, frighten her, or threaten her, I will take action and I guarantee you won't like it."

The thug, having had a few hours to sober up, and consider what he had done, seemed to realize what an ass he had made of himself. He promised.

"You really think it'll be okay?" Janice mumbled to Gus when he returned to the station.

"Don't give it another thought," he said. "Try not to worry."

"That's easier said than done, Gus, He scared me."

"I'm sure he did," he said. "I'm sorry about the whole thing."

*****

The offer was $400,000 for the mineral rights; or if the Sioux wished to sell the (Black) Hills outright the price would be six million dollars payable in 15 annual installments. This was a markdown price indeed, considering that one Black Hills mine alone yielded more than 500 million dollars in gold.

--Brown, D. *Bury My Heart at Wounded Knee*. P. 284

CHAPTER NINE

She walked into her job at the Inn the next morning and headed to the service locker room. She changed into her maid uniform and refreshed her makeup. The room was empty as she turned to go, but her supervisor opened the door.

"Hi Janice," Gayle said. "Glad I caught you. You have a present waiting for you at the main desk."

Puzzled, Janice walked into the office and found an elaborate bouquet of roses on the counter. She gasped at seeing them. "These are for me?" she asked.

"They certainly are," said Mrs. Ross, the supervisor. "Here's the card."

Janice took the card. Her name was written on it in black marker. There was no signature on the card.

"Was this all that came with it?" she asked Mrs. Ross.

"Yep," nodded the woman. "That's a lovely bouquet."

Puzzled, Janice gained permission to leave the roses in the office until she was finished with work. "Absolutely," said Mrs. Ross. The secretarial staff nodded with enthusiasm. The roses, clearly fresh, had given the drab office a dash of color and a delightful scent.

Janice fought through the distraction of the lovely gift as she worked on the rooms. She had a British literature class that afternoon and struggled to focus on Ode on a Grecian Urn by Keats and She Walks in Beauty by Lord Byron. She loved the study of the Romantic Poets, and poetry in general, but she felt dragged away.

Who would have sent her roses?

It had to be Ron. He'd had a chance to think over the conversation from the last night they'd been together. Sure. He'd realized that he'd been short with her. Sure.

But no. No, that couldn't be it. They'd broken things off a few months ago. They weren't going to see one another again…

She tried some names out. Gus, the gas station owner. No, of course not. Such a gift would be woefully inappropriate, right?

Her ex-husband? Ridiculous. Well, he was still her husband technically, to be sure. They hadn't signed any papers. Still he was furious with her. There was no chance he'd send flowers.

She ran over some other men she'd met, or gotten to know, but she could think of no one who would have sent such an extravagant gift.

The class ended, and Dr. Wilkie, the professor, called her aside. "I don't want to pry," he said. "I saw that you were distracted today."

"Oh," she said. "I'm sorry. Nothing's wrong. Well, there is, but…"

"I get it," Dr. Wilkie smiled. "It's nothing that concerns me."

"I don't mean that at all," she said. "Thank you for your interest. It really means a lot to me. It's just that something strange happened to me this morning, and I don't know what to make of it."

"Janice," he said, and she was surprised that he'd called her by her first name. Usually, the professors called her Mrs. O'Neill. "I am going to trust you that you would tell me if you are in any danger."

She thought for a little bit. "No," she said. "At least, I haven't felt threatened. I so appreciate your concern, Professor Wilkie."

"Okay," he replied. "I'll trust that you'll let me know if you want to talk or need some help."

She considered. "Thanks, Professor Wilkie."

She left the room and retreated to the office at the Inn, where she collected her flowers. She asked the secretary if she'd seen Ron recently. The secretary frowned and squinted in thought.

"No, I haven't," she said. "We haven't heard from him." Janice peered into the mailbox that still retained Ron's name for some reason, but found it empty. The secretary shrugged. "No idea."

Feeling awkward, Janice asked to use the office phone. She dialed Ron's office and then his home phone number. She received a disconnect message at each number.

She puzzled about this as she climbed into her car. She hadn't dated anyone for quite a while.

But, there was no return address. No forwarding address. No phone numbers!

*****

(1878) The force was gone out of the Cheyennes. In the years since the massacre at Sand Creek, doom had stalked the beautiful people. The seed of the tribe was scattered with the wind…Soon there would be no one left who could care enough to remember, no one to speak their names now that they were gone.

--Brown, Dee. p. 349.

Chapter Ten

Janice sat on the edge of her cot that night and wept, feeling lonely and sorry for herself. Now what? Life wasn't really working out too well. Her thoughts turned, as they frequently did, to her daughters, living with the man who would soon be her ex-husband.

As always happened, a wave of guilt swept over her. To be honest, she didn't exactly miss the girls. Nonetheless she felt that she had abandoned her responsibility with her daughters and stuck her ex-husband with her failure.

She didn't have time to grieve, she decided. She had to push it away. She had final exams starting on Monday, and she needed to do well. She picked up a copy of Blake's poetry and began to read.

*****

In the morning she felt better, as she had expected. The responsibilities of her jobs caught up with her at once and she blasted off to work. She lost herself in cleaning and freshening the hotel rooms. When she had finished, she grabbed a quick bite to eat at a Shoney's, and then hustled to the gas station and a tune-up on a Chevy.

To her gratification the engine began to purr as she changed plugs, set the new points, changed the fluids and the filters and greased up the car. As she finished she felt a good deal of satisfaction at having done a job well. The car ran as well as it had when it was brand new.

The car's owner came in as she was finishing, and was

pleased at how well the car was running. "May I suggest we add a can of STP?" she said. "There's still a little balk, and I think it's just a carbon buildup." The owner agreed, and Janice poured in the additive.

"It should be fine now, Mr. Coulter," she told him. He paid the bill with some good cheer.

Gus went home about 8:00, leaving her in charge as he had extended the hours since her arrival. He took the day's receipts to the bank and left her with just enough change to finish the shift before bed.

She sat at the stool behind the counter, pulled out her notes from the British Literature class and began to study. She continued to study until she couldn't read any more.

She rose, turned out the lights, the gas pumps and the lights in the service bays. Back to her room—

And then, she began to cry. O God, what now? She prayed, and felt that she was saying prayers that went no further than the ceiling and walls of the station office. What do I do now? She asked herself, not really expecting a response.

But then the door opened.

*****

A tall man, wearing a trench coat and sunglasses, stood in the doorway to her room at the back of the gas station. She had cleaned and painted the room so that it didn't smell of gasoline, old oil and solvents. It was close to being bright and cheerful. Still, it was a room in the back of a gas station.

"May I come in?" he asked.

"The station is closed," Janice said, an almost automatic response. She didn't feel scared.

"I don't need gasoline," smiled the man. A glow came from

him, she saw, and she relaxed almost at once. He took off his trench coat and his sunglasses. She now saw his eyes were a peculiar color: not brown, but more golden. He lifted his arms and stretched them out to her.

Janice, to her complete surprise, took two quick steps and fell into his embrace. She began crying in the next few moments and stayed for some time just relaxing in his embrace.

"My name is Curiel, Janice," said the man.

"Yes," she said. "I feel like I know you."

"Beloved," he said. "You have some serious difficulties, don't you."

"Curiel, what do I do?"

"You need to come to grips with who you are, Beloved," he explained. "You need to clear away some of the wounds in your life."

"Wounds?" said Janice.

"You still resent your father," he continued.

"No, of course I don't," she said. "I…" she fell silent. She couldn't look up.

"When you were sleeping with those men," he said, and now Janice began to cry. He paused. "I know, Beloved. You are not really that person. You were taking revenge." She considered.

"Your father was distant when you were young, and took little interest in you," he went on. Even now Janice couldn't disagree. "And then both he and your mother died. You felt deserted."

"Yes, I think so," she agreed. "After they both died in that car accident, I guess I did resent not having a mom and dad like all the other kids at school. I had to change schools and go live with my grandmother and grandfather who loved me and tried really hard but it was just not the same."

"Can you finish your bachelor's degree soon?" he asked, though she was certain he already knew the answer.

"Yes, if I put…" she hesitated.

"If you put your mind to it?" he added.

"Yes," she agreed.

"I can't help you with this," he said.

"I think I understand," she whispered. "You can't do anything for me that I have to do for myself."

"Correct," he said.

"Okay," she nodded. "So I'll see you in a month or two, right?"

"Finish your degree," he said, and then he wasn't there.

Following his visit, Janice became even more serious about her schoolwork. She wrote the papers, took the tests, and finished her bachelor's degree within two years despite working full time. For the first time in her life she felt a sense of true accomplishment.

She took the diploma from the hand of the chancellor of the University and ran down the steps. She found Curiel waiting for her. She went to him and they hugged. Opening the diploma, she pointed to a gold sticker on the front of the degree.

"Cum Laude," she said. "Curiel, I graduated with honors."

"Excellent, Beloved," he congratulated. "No one can take that diploma away from you."

"I know," she said, glowing with pride. "Now the University wants me to continue into their Master's program."

"And?" his eyes twinkled.

"You want me to do my best, don't you?" she asked, but it

was far more an assertion than a question.

"Yes, I do, Beloved," he agreed. "You need to be devoted to excellence now and for the rest of your life. You feel, as you should, a desire to be the best at what you do, am I not correct?"

Janice thought. Then she hugged him. "I promise to do the best I can, Curiel. At everything." Curiel vanished.

*****

The Poncas of Indian Territory had learned a bitter lesson. The white man's law was illusion; it did not apply to them. And so, like the Cheyenne, the diminishing Ponca tribe was split in two. Standing Bear's band free in the south, the others prisoners in the north country.

--Brown, p. 36

CHAPTER ELEVEN

Two years passed, and Janice earned a Master's degree, then completed the course work on a Doctorate, and found herself mulling her future. She still had a year or two to go to complete her doctorate, since she needed to write her dissertation.

She had received several teaching offers, which intrigued her, but she found herself not wanting to commit to something immediately.

On the contrary, Janice wanted to travel and see more than the southern tier of The United States. She found that she wanted to meet people around the world and expand her horizons. Her problem was that she had very little money left from her college savings, even with her scholarships and grants from the University.

She applied and was accepted for a job as a flight attendant with American Airlines, and within six months she had an exciting position. Serving people came naturally to her and she did very well. It was difficult to resign from the gas station, and Gus expressed his disappointment. Still, he acknowledged that she needed to move along with her life and gave her a graduation gift, a beautiful leather suitcase embossed with her initials.

She decided to put her education on hold for a while and took a break from her doctoral studies, working for an hour or so at a time. She worked and made progress on the dissertation, but her job fascinated her and made her happy. It was a nice change from the academic discipline in which she'd spent her last few years.

On occasion, she would receive invitations to dinner with men she would meet on the plane. Once in a while, she'd accept the invitations and have enjoyable evenings. Though she liked many of the men, as a rule she wouldn't accept invitations to second dates. She knew that a few of them would have been interested in pursuing more than casual friendships, and in a few instances, may have even wanted to become serious to the point of marriage.

But Janice could not consider romance. She didn't think she had the strength to fight off advances, nor did she want to hurt the mood of a pleasant evening. As a flight attendant she was able to enjoy some of the most beautiful and famous cities across America.

Then one night she had dinner with an interesting man from Nashville. The next day she had a layover, and arranged to spend the day with the man, whose name was Erik.

She took a cab to his hotel, the Gaylord Opryland & Convention Center, not far from the site of the Opryland Amusement park. He had rented a car and took her into Nashville, where they toured Centennial Park, The Parthenon, and many other wonderful tourist sights, in the lovely city. They had dinner at a great restaurant, Fleming's Prime Steakhouse & Wine Bar. Her steak was the finest she'd ever had, and he ordered a superb California Burgundy to compliment the beef, the delicate shrimp appetizer and the salad.

Janice, a girl from a small town in North Carolina, had never eaten and enjoyed such a marvelous meal. He invited her to his hotel after dinner, and rather to her surprise, she accepted.

The sex was long, slow and delicious. He proved himself to

be a considerate, skillful lover. Her life had been chaste for several years, and the evening was something of a revelation.

When she woke up in his hotel room the next morning, she found him lying next to her, smiling down at her. She stretched and felt the pleasant soreness that accompanies fine sex. He'd been wonderful, and to her surprise she realized that she felt no guilt, no remorse, and no reservations about her conduct.

"Damn," she uttered, and realized she hadn't said anything even resembling profanity for several years. She apologized, and he laughed.

"That was a wonderful evening," she said. "Why?"

He gave her a puzzled smile. "Why what?" he asked.

"Why did you spend that much money on me?" she asked.

Now he laughed out loud. "Don't you know the expression 'Snow Job'?" he asked.

She whacked his chest. "I wouldn't have cost that much anyhow," she said. "You could have had me a lot cheaper."

They began making love again, and she felt again the profound warm pleasure that comes with using one's body to thank and express joy in another person.

Forty-five minutes later they were in the elevator, headed down to the lobby and the coffee shop. After a solid, not to say lavish breakfast, she said, "Can I ask a question?"

He didn't look pleased, but he did nod. "Sure," he said.

"First: are you married?"

He grimaced. "I figured that would be the first question. The answer is complex. In some ways, yes, I am. My wife and I live in separate homes: I in Sacramento, she in Cleveland."

"Why don't you divorce?" she asked.

His answer was a shrug. "There's a good answer," he said.

"But it's complicated."

She sat back, folded her napkin and said, "Well, if things had been different last night, I would have said, 'I guess it's none of my business."

He considered that. "I'm not exactly sure I know what you mean."

"I don't know a great deal about sex," said Janice. "Indeed, I'm an amateur. But I do know that something major transpired in that bed last night. I think we both felt a genuine connection."

"You didn't think it was just casual sex?" smiled Erik. She shook her head.

"No, I certainly don't," she asserted. "If it had been merely casual, we would never have spent as much time doing things to give the other person pleasure."

"Do you mind being more—ah—specific?"

"A mere sexual encounter would have involved far less attention to detail. You let it go on much longer than I even considered."

"And you responded by—"

"Doing far more than I ever did before."

He nodded. "Why did you extend yourself as you did?"

She sat up straight and composed an answer. "I realized that I really needed far more from the encounter than I have before."

"I don't..." he began.

"I made a hash of my marriage," she continued. "It was a disaster."

"But we're not married," he said. "I wouldn't, and didn't, suggest we get married or even hint at it."

"I know," she said. "It was mostly on my part, I think. I wanted to know how you were responding to me. When I extended myself, I felt you give back to me. I felt you pushing yourself to be the best lover that you could be with me."

"Is that what married people do?" smiled her friend.

"I think so," said Janice. "I also think I could do that for you every time I made love to you."

"Do you mean that?" he said, his voice sober.

She swallowed. She hadn't intended to go that far. But, she realized, she meant it.

"Yes," she said. "But I'm afraid I couldn't do it again right now. Or any time soon, either."

His mouth dropped open. "Are you kidding?" he stumbled. "We've been enjoying one of the best evenings either one of us have ever had, haven't we?"

"I can't deny that," she said. "Nor would I want to. I've loved every minute of being with you. It has been wonderful. But sex is for married people."

"I tend to agree," he said. "But we really can't get married."

"Not with you already married," she agreed.

"That's a big consideration," he said.

"That is the consideration," she emphasized. "While you try to make up your mind about wanting to be with me, my life is passing. Yes, the sex went well and would continue. But I can't get pregnant, I can't build a life around you, or invest in this area, without you."

"Look at it this way," he began.

"I think it's better if we end it now, right here," she said, not sure where she was getting the words she was saying. "I have a night coach flight tonight, and I have to get to New York. I'll be gone for several days."

"Janice, you're being silly—"

"Probably," she agreed. Then she went through the coffee shop door and into the street. She hailed a cab and went to the hotel where she'd parked her rental car. She never heard from the man again.

*****

The Army conquered the Sioux. You can order them around. But we Utes have never disturbed you whites. So, you must wait until we come to your way of thinking.

--Brown, p. 367

CHAPTER TWELVE

When Janice returned to the airport in her hometown, she climbed into her car and started it up. She drove home toward the little apartment that she'd rented after her years in the back of the gas station. She turned left onto the main street…

When she straightened the wheel, she found Curiel sitting next to her. Her friend would just show up sometimes, and let her bounce things off him. It startled her for just a second until she realized who he was.

"You are not happy with this lifestyle, are you?" asked her friend.

She weighed her answer. "No," she agreed. "I'm certainly not. I'm lonely, despite my job—"

"You meet a lot of people as a flight attendant," observed the Angel.

"Yes, I do," she agreed. "Erik seemed very nice, didn't he?"

"But he really wasn't, was he?" said Curiel.

She didn't answer but looked out the window into the street.

"Have you considered what you will do should you become pregnant by one of these men?"

Well, it hadn't completely escaped her notice. She kept some foam contraceptive with her, a sponge that had never failed, and which yet seemed not to interfere.

"I haven't been careless, have I?" she answered, a bit more sharply than she intended.

"Indeed, not yet," he agreed. "But there is still a substantial risk. Also, you are risking disease, very crippling and potentially fatal, are you not?"

Now, her tears began to fall. "Have I ever done one thing right?" she asked.

"Yes," he said. "You established a covenant with the One who can protect you for eternity. Perhaps you recall going forward at a tent revival meeting when you were in seventh grade."

"Of course, I remember," she murmured. "But that didn't make my grandparents happy. They did not understand since they followed the old Indian ways."

"Was that response typical," he asked.

"No, they were kind and loving but I was rebellious and rejected the Indian beliefs as a teen-ager. I just wanted to fit in with all the kids at school," she explained. She choked on the memory and she wiped a tear from her cheek.

A Piggly Wiggly lot came into view and she pulled the car into a remote spot so that she could cry until the storm passed in her soul.

Curiel reached across the bench seat and took her hand. She leaned toward him, sobbing and coughing, and he embraced her. "Oh Curiel," she cried. "I've made such a hash of things."

"Yet you did the right thing, didn't you?"

"What do you mean?" she managed.

"I mean, you walked away from that man," he said. "You did not let yourself be further humiliated."

"But..." she began, and then choked on the answer.

"Few marriages based in adultery thrive, Beloved," he said.

"Really?" she sobbed.

"Of course," he said. "The most precious and sincere vows you ever took were in front of the pastor who performed your marriage. Since then, you have given in to the flattery of men who found you attractive. You all but destroyed your husband."

"Should I have stayed with him?" she asked.

He shook his head. "I do not know, and cannot tell you," he said. "Even if I did know, I would not tell you. No one is ever told what would have happened. What I do know is that you once took a marriage vow and you have dishonored it. You have received all the guidance you need and you could have divined the truth with an appropriate amount of study."

A handkerchief-like cloth appeared in his hand, and he told her to keep it. Her tears began to settle down. The cloth seemed to have peculiar warmth, imparting healing, comfort, and love. She kept the cloth with her for the rest of her life and it would become an heirloom in her family.

He released her at last and she leaned back against the seat. "Now what do I do?" she asked, still feeling wretched, but clinging to the comforting hand of a friend—her best friend, she decided. Maybe her only friend.

"Make good decisions, Precious," he said. "Like you did today. Don't marry because you are lonely. In this case the physical aspect was delightful, but you didn't connect spiritually, emotionally, or mentally. You were ready to commit without knowing him."

She considered. "Is that what I did with my husband?"

"You have to answer that, Beloved," he said. "Marry, on the contrary, when you meet the right man. You have the wisdom to know who he is."

"I guess—" she began, but hesitated as a new thought occurred. "I was looking to replace my father, wasn't I"

"Yes," said Curiel. "You never believed you were capable of

living and surviving on your own."

"I've always had a hard time believing in myself, haven't I?"

"Well?" He smiled. "How did you do with your college work?"

"I did well."

"How about at the gas station, and your flight attendant work as well?"

"I did very well most of the time."

"So," said the Angel, embracing her. "Is there any indication that you won't do well with the rest of your life?"

She thought for a second, but then shook her head.

"Focus on growing in the four aspects of your life, Beloved."

"I promise."

"Farewell, Beloved," said her friend. And then he wasn't there.

*****

(1889) Before Sitting Bull could get away from the grounds, a newspaperman asked him how the Indians felt about giving up their lands. "Indians!" Sitting Bull shouted. "There are no Indians left but me!"

--Brown, Dee. p. 178

CHAPTER THIRTEEN

The next morning Janice drove to Gus' Gas Station, parked her car and went in. Gus looked up, and beamed when he realized who it was. "Well, well," he said. "The princess of Chapel Hill." She laughed. "To what may I count myself indebted for this visit to my humble station?"

"I don't know," she shrugged, delighted to see this good friend. "Slumming, I think they used to call it."

They chuckled together. "Look what I just got in," he said. He tossed her a small wrapped package.

She looked and gave him a high five. "Chuckles," she said, unwrapping the candy. "My favorite."

"I know," he said.

She shook the little rectangles onto the counter. "You want the licorice, of course?" she asked her former boss. He held out his hand. She tossed it to him and held up the red candy in a little toast.

He pulled up a chair for her on the opposite side of the desk and they sat. She brought him up to date on her work, and told him about some of the places she'd visited.

"I scored a couple of trips to Hawaii last month," she said. "It's unusual, I know, but one of the girls got sick. No, it was in coach, not first-class seating. It was non-stop, straight through from Chicago-O'Hare to Honolulu."

"You went to Oahu?" he asked, envious.

"Yeah, but I had a two-day layover and hopped over to Maui," she said. She told him about staying in Kaanapali for a couple of nights before having to return to Honolulu for the flight back.

"But still no romance?" he teased.

"No," she laughed. "I met a man and we were doing okay, I thought, but it turned out he was married."

"Ouch," he said, giving a little wince.

"Yeah, no kidding," she said. "I told him I didn't want to see him again."

They chatted for about a half hour, interrupted from time to time by customers pulling in and out, cigarette and candy purchases. "You remember the Walcott kids?" Gus asked.

"Sure," she groaned, not enjoying the memory of a family of violent delinquents. "I used to have to run one or the other of them out of here several times a week."

"I know," he said. "One of them, the one named Rufus, came in here a few minutes before you showed up. He said that his dad had sent him over to buy him a pack of cigarettes."

"Jeez," said Janice. "How old is he, twelve or so?"

"I think about there," agreed Gus. "He's awful young to start smoking, don't you think?"

"You didn't sell the cigarettes to him, did you?" she smiled.

"Hell no," he scoffed. "I told him to tell his Dad to buy his own cigarettes, the lazy slob."

"My ex-husband was a teacher," she reminded him, and he nodded. "He'd come home with stories all the time about kids trying to get away with things. He said that one time he was talking to a freshman who was doing a week of detention. He asked him why."

"Again, with the thinking he's smarter than the school, right?"

"There was a room in the gym where they stored mats and physical education equipment," Janice continued. "The room was never locked. Every year, they'd have kids trying to hide out in there to skip out of classes, or an assembly. They'd think they were the first to ever come up with the plan."

"Criminy," he said, and turned to a customer who'd come into the station. The bell rang as a black Cadillac pulled up to the pump outside.

"Want me to get that, Gus?" she asked.

"Sure, if you don't mind," he shrugged.

Janice walked out to the Cadillac and greeted the customer, who requested a fill-up with Premium. The customer recognized her and struck up a little conversation with her. "When you coming back?" he asked. "I never trust anyone but you to change my oil."

She laughed, processed his credit card, and gave him the receipt. She then attended to five other customers, one after another, smiling and joking, enjoying the interaction with the people.

At last she walked back into the station and again sat down with Gus. "Just like old times?" he asked.

"You know, I enjoyed that," she confessed. "It was kind of fun, sure."

"You looking for a job?" he asked.

"I wasn't," she shrugged.

"It's yours if you want it," he said. "I'm pretty sure you don't want the store room again—" she groaned and nodded— "but you could work a few days a week, or whatever you wanted. It works for me. People like having you around and you're good for business."

"I fly two or three days a week," she said. "Could you be flexible?"

She agreed to work when she could, and to abide by whatever schedule they wanted to set up. She liked the job, of course, and a bit of extra income would not come amiss. Sure, it would be minimum wage but…

Three months later, Gus' business had improved to the point that he gave her a significant raise. He was elated by the way old customers had been returning, and Janice was delighted to help out her old friend who had been so kind to her in some of the most desperate hours of her life. He made it easy to accept a second job where she could use her mechanical gifts.

She went on occasional dates, and some of the men were attractive and fun to be with. She renewed her friendships at the station and business continued to improve. She avoided serious involvements, not wanting to make any permanent commitments, just not able to extend herself physically to another person.

And then, the flower deliveries began again.

*****

They made us many promises, more than I can remember, but they never kept but one; they promised to take our land, and they took it.

--Oglala Sioux War Chief Red Cloud (Mahpiua-luta),
Bury My Heart at Wounded Knee, p. 109.

Chapter Fourteen

Janice knew something was up when she came in to the gas station about four o'clock one Friday afternoon. She'd had a back and forth flight from Chapel Hill to Chicago, then to Newark, back to Chicago and ended at Chapel Hill. She did this run occasionally and had to struggle to be patient and pleasant.

"Hey," said Gus. "Tough day?" he asked, seeing her weariness.

"Ah," she said. "I'll be okay, once I finish the shift tonight. I'm going straight home, though."

"Right," he said. "Oh—ah—These came for you. About a half hour ago."

He pulled a dozen long stem roses from behind the counter and laid them on the glass next to the cash register. "This card was with it," he added.

Janice, a bit nervous, opened the little envelope. A small card inside paid her an innocuous compliment, but she found no signature.

Janice stepped to the phone and called the Florist who had delivered them. "Dave," she said when Dave the Florist, a regular customer at the gas station, answered. "This is Janice at Gus' Standard."

"Hey, Angel," said the Florist, and she could hear the smile in his voice. "Did you like the bouquet?"

"Of course, I do," she said. "But there was no signature."

"Well, I just assumed you knew who sent them," he said. "I wasn't concerned. Should I be?"

"Do you know who sent them?" she asked.

"Well, no," he said. "I didn't see any name on the order. It was a cash purchase. You mean you don't know who sent them to you?"

"No, I don't, Dave," she said. "This hasn't happened for a few years, since I've been away."

"Oh Jeez, I hope it didn't scare you," he said.

"Not scare, but concern," she said. "I didn't know who sent them several years ago. I don't know who sent them today, and I don't know how he knew I'd be here to pick them up."

"Oh, jeez," he repeated. "Did Gus have your phone number?"

She thought. "Yes, I've kept the same number since I moved here years ago. It hasn't changed."

"Well," said Dave the Florist. "I guess the person figured that Gus would know how to get hold of you, right?"

"Hmm," she said.

"I've never heard of someone stalking a person with flowers," said Dave. "Look, do you want me not to send the flowers again if I get an order?"

She hesitated. "I guess if you don't send them, he'll get someone else, right? Another flower shop?"

"Have you contacted the police?" Dave asked.

"And say what?" she said with a shrug. "Someone's sending me flowers?"

He chuckled. "Well, my cousin's a cop here in town. Why don't I set up an informal meet for you?"

Janice thought for a second, and then agreed. A car came in to the station and she rang off with the florist to go and take care of the motorist.

*****

"It will be a very hard thing to leave the country that God gave us," Little Raven said. "Our friends are buried there, and we hate to leave these grounds."

--Little Raven, War Chief of the Northern Cheyenne, *Bury My Heart at Wounded Knee*, p. 100

CHAPTER FIFTEEN

The next morning, a tall man in a sport shirt and tie walked into the station. Janice asked if she could help him.

"You Janice?" he smiled.

"I'm the only woman here, so yes," she said, grinning.

"I'm Jim Kruger," he said, and flashed a badge and identification.

"Oh, you're Dave the Florist's cousin, right?"

"Yeah, Jim the cop. Understand things are a bit strange, huh?"

"I can't even file a complaint," she explained. "I guess I just needed to talk to a policeman. I'm getting nervous."

"Tell me," Kruger said.

She told about how she'd started working at the gas station and then began receiving flowers, never with a signature card. No, she told him, the shops never knew who ordered them.

"How can that be?" he asked.

"Every shop I talked to said that a boy, a different one every time, came in and paid cash for the flowers. He'd hand the owner or the clerk a note—no, never handwritten—and pay cash for the roses and delivery."

"How many times did this happen?" frowned Kruger.

"Off and on, for practically the whole time I worked here," she responded.

"And then it started up again yesterday?"

"This is the strangest thing," she continued. "I didn't know I was even going to come in here. I haven't worked here since I've been in school—I got a bachelor's and master's degree over the last several years—except to buy gas when I was in the neighborhood."

"Hmm," he said. "The perp must have figured out how to find you."

"I suppose. He always seemed to know when I'd be here, though."

"You're assuming it's a 'he', are you?"

"Yes," she said. "It hasn't occurred to me to think anything else."

"Have you felt that you're being followed? Any notes, phone calls?"

Janice, feeling close to tears, shook her head.

He paused. "I don't see a crime here, at least not one that's actionable." He glanced down at his notepad and wrote something.

"Does scaring me badly count?" she snapped, her tone more than a bit sharp.

He looked up. "Of course, it does. I apologize if I sounded callous and uncaring."

Janice dabbed her eyes. Again, he apologized.

"It's a question of prosecution, though. Even if I find him, what jury would convict someone for sending flowers to an attractive woman, in particular because you haven't been threatened, you haven't seen the person, received anything other than flowers—"

"I see," she mumbled. "But am I in danger?"

He hesitated. Then, "Have you considered moving to another part of the country?"

She stared at him for a second or two. "Well, yes I have," she assented. "I was seeing a man who moved to Washington State and he wanted me to come with him, but that was before all these deliveries started."

"Didn't work out, I assume," said the cop.

"No, it was quite a while ago. I regret it in some ways, but I certainly couldn't have gone with him. I wasn't divorced at that point. It was still in the process."

"You are divorced now?"

"Yes, and my ex remarried."

They talked for several more moments, but Jim at last said, "Mrs. O'Neill, I don't have a lot to go on here, but I'll look into things." He handed her a couple of business cards. "Look, if you get scared, or you get more of these flower deliveries, let me know, and I'll be in touch. I'll try to work backwards on this."

The bell for the gas pumps rang, and Janice said goodbye to the detective who promised to stay in touch. She resumed her chores at the station, but she felt distracted the rest of the day.

"Who would be stalking me?" she wondered out loud. Gus, who was doing a major valve job on an old Chevy, looked up.

"Said what?" he asked.

She shook her head. "Didn't mean to say that out loud."

"Look," he said. "If you need some time…"

"No, that's not it," she said. "I guess I just have to get used to feeling scared." She told him that the detective had suggested that she re-locate to another part of the country.

"It's a thought," he agreed. "I'd hate to have you go. It's fun having a flight attendant working as a mechanic, I have to say—"

"Oh give me a break," she sighed. "Right. The height of glamour." He laughed and ducked under the hood of the car again.

****

This war did not spring up here in our land; this war was brought upon us by the children of the Great Father who came to take our land from us without price and who, in our land, do a great many evil things…it has been our wish to live here in our country peaceably…

--Sinte-Galeshka (Chief Spotted Tail) of the Brule Sioux. *Bury My Heart at Wounded Knee*, p. 122

Chapter Sixteen

A few minutes later, the bell rang in the station and Janice went outside to pump the gas. "Fill it up, please," said the man, who wore huge sunglasses even though the day was cloudy.

"Sure," she said. "Premium?"

"Yeah," said the man.

Janice started the pump and then it occurred to her. The voice sounded familiar. The man hadn't been anyone she recognized at first, but she thought that she recognized the peculiar rasp in the voice. She had a strong impression that the voice was that of someone she'd seen before.

Janice cleaned the glass on the car, and asked if she could check under the hood. The man stared at her for a few moments and the stare became uncomfortable as the seconds ticked past. At last he said, "Thank you, that won't be necessary."

Again, the voice. Again, the surety that she'd heard it before. The man handed her his credit card, and she retreated to the station. The name on the card wasn't familiar.

"Gus," she said.

"Yeah," said her boss, as he came into the office wiping his hands on a red rag.

"Take a look at this card," she said.

"Something wrong?" he asked as he examined the card.

"I don't know," she said. "I just have a really funny feeling about this guy. Like I've seen him before."

"I'll take the card reader back to him," he offered. "Let me get a look."

She handed the card reader to him. She walked into the first repair bay and watched as he handed the device to the man. He signed it and Gus returned to the station as the man started the car and drove away. Gus handed her the credit card reader. It had the name of the motorist written on it. Janice shrugged and said she didn't recognize it.

"He didn't look familiar, exactly," Gus said. "Did he scare you?"

"I don't think he scared me," she said. "But I am puzzled. At first I thought I knew his voice. But then I couldn't be sure."

Gus smiled. "Well, he's gone, now. Don't worry about it."

*****

Roman Nose was dead; Black Kettle was dead; Tall Bull was dead. Now they were all 'good Indians.' Like the antelope, and the buffalo, the ranks of the proud Cheyenne were thinning into extinction.

--*Bury My Heart at Wounded Knee*, p. 174

CHAPTER SEVENTEEN

The phone rang early the next morning. Janice struggled awake and fumbled for the receiver. "Hello?" she mumbled.

"Janice," said the voice. She recognized the caller at once.

"Hi Marianne," she said. "Don't tell me."

"Right," said Marianne, her supervisor. "Can you take an L. A. run today?"

"Sure, I guess so," she muttered.

"You have to be at the AP in two hours," said Marianne. "Still okay?"

"Over night?" asked Janice.

"Yeah, 'fraid so," said her boss.

"Okay," she said. She called Gus, and apologized. He told her not to worry about it.

"See you in a couple of days," she said.

An hour later Janice arrived at Raleigh-Durham International and boarded the shuttle to Atlanta. She had time to store her luggage and then helped settle the passengers. The flight wasn't completely full, and a few standbys came in.

She helped the passengers store their luggage and belted herself in. The flight took off on time for the short hop to Atlanta. The flight had a beverage service, which the service crew administered.

Janice was storing the soft drinks when Julie, her partner, came over. "Do you know the guy in seat 10A?" she asked. "The one with the heavy beard and baseball cap?"

Janice looked out. She saw a man sitting and working a crossword puzzle in the seat Julie had indicated. "No," she said.

"I don't think so. Why?"

"He told me to say hi to you," said Julie.

Janice, when she had a second, walked back to the seat in question. "Did you say hello to me, sir?" she asked.

He looked up. "Yes, I've flown with you before."

Again, the voice was peculiar, raspy. "What run, sir?"

"I think I went with you to New York, if I'm not mistaken," he smiled.

Well, he didn't seem threatening. "Thanks for remembering," she said, returning his smile. "Where are you heading today?"

"Atlanta," he said. "Then I'll return later this evening."

"I'm going with this crew on to Los Angeles," she added. "I won't be back for a day or two. I envy you."

"You seem to like your job, though," he said.

"Yes, I do. I have another job. I didn't get home until late last night, and then I had to shoot over to R-D for this flight."

"Perhaps a nap later?" he suggested.

"We'll see. It's a living." He smiled, and gave a laugh.

He'd been polite and friendly, she thought as she walked back to the service area.

By the time the jet took off headed to L. A., she'd made an effort to put the meeting with the man on the plane behind her. After the service cart was finished and put away, she'd forgotten about him.

The plane landed in Los Angeles in the early afternoon. As she and the rest of the flight crew traveled to the hotel for the evening, however, she thought again about the man.

It was strange, she thought. She had no memory whatsoever of seeing him on a flight.

That night Janice shared a room with Susan, another flight attendant from her crew. They stayed at the airport hotel and had dinner at an unpretentious restaurant. She felt a little troubled about the encounter on the plane with the man who claimed to know her. "Susan," she began. "Did you see that guy in 10A on our first leg to Atlanta?"

Susan looked up. "What guy in 10A?"

"Cheryl said a guy in 10A wanted to talk to me."

Susan frowned. "No one sat in 10A for that flight."

"What?" said Janice.

"Yeah," Susan said. "I served that row. No one was there."

And Janice felt cold.

*****

When the Civil War began, (Ely Samuel) Parker returned to New York with plans to raise a regiment of Iroquois Indians to fight for the Union. His request for permission to do so was turned down by the governor, who told him bluntly that he had no place for Indians in the New York Volunteers. "Go home, cultivate your farm, and we will settle our own troubles without any Indian aid."

--Brown, p. 179.

CHAPTER EIGHTEEN

The flight back to O'Hare the next morning was uneventful. A husband and wife came aboard and Janice noticed that they were dressed in virtually identical outfits.

"Are you two twins?" she grinned as they came aboard.

"No," said the husband with a smile.

"But we have been married for forty years," laughed the wife. "I guess that's why we look so much alike."

The three chuckled together. Later, Janice took complimentary glasses of wine to the couple for being good sports. They thanked her and told her they were enjoying the flight.

The flight landed on time at O'Hare, and Janice sat in the crew lounge with a newspaper for an hour before boarding an Atlanta shuttle. The flight was only half full, and Janice went back to the empty last row and fell asleep in moments. One of the attendants awoke her in Atlanta and she made her way to the shuttle for Raleigh-Durham. The flight crew greeted her and asked if she could help serve the flight.

"You short here?" she asked.

"Yeah," said the chief flight attendant. "We need one more. One of the girls got sick at our last stop."

"I get it," nodded Janice.

The flight took off on time and again the plane was rather empty. The flight had a beverage service and Janice helped in coach.

She noted that seat 10A was unoccupied on this flight. She felt relief. Susan's assertion that the seat had been unoccupied on the way to Atlanta had spooked her. She returned to the kitchen after the service run and secured the cart.

The flight entered Raleigh-Durham airspace a few moments later and Janice buckled herself in for the landing in a seat at the rear of the plane. She looked forward into the plane.

Someone was now sitting in 10A. He wore an Atlanta Braves hat, she noticed.

"Sammy," she said to the attendant sitting next to her. "Do you see someone sitting in 10A?"

Samantha looked up. "10A?" she asked. She looked at the seat as the plane's wheels hit the ground and the plane began to decelerate.   She turned and peered at Janice. "No one's there, Janice."

Janice looked again. Samantha was right. What on earth is happening? She thought. Samantha consulted the passenger list. "No one's booked in that seat, Janice."

Janice sat back and waited for the plane to stop. She and Samantha went forward when the plane stopped at the gate. Janice couldn't resist looking at 10A. No one was there.

She helped the crew unload the passengers, struggling to smile and say goodbye.

She watched each passenger as closely as she could to see if any of them were wearing or carrying an Atlanta Braves baseball hat. No, she saw no one.

"Could I have hallucinated this guy?"

Janice needed to clear her head. She went into the terminal. A flight was just boarding for Rio de Janeiro, and she managed to get a seat. Anything to get out of there with as much haste as possible.

The flight went well, and Janice found a hotel near the Ocean, bordering on Copacabana Beach. After checking in, she rented a chair and took a large towel from the hotel. She went to a shop on the beach and bought a mind-numbing bikini. "I've never worn anything like this," she told the clerk.

"You will stun the men at the beach," said the clerk, smiling as she wrote it up.

"You promise?" she said, and the clerk grinned. She also purchased a pair of swim goggles, not wanting to spend the night with irritated eyes. She changed into the bikini in the shop, and strolled down to the beach.

The bikini had the predicted effect. She felt a bit self-conscious and shy at first, but she found herself enjoying the stares she received at the beach. It was good for her ego.

Janice spent a few days on the beautiful beach, tanning, dozing in the sun, reading a couple of novels she'd been meaning to get to. The books were somewhat routine, she felt, and her mind returned again and again to her night in the Nashville hotel room. She'd had a wonderful dinner, a delightful evening, and then she slept with him—

"Why did I tell him that I wanted to marry him?" she thought aloud.

The answer came: You wanted to make sure he knew that you were willing to be his failsafe. He didn't want any commitment. As he had talked that night, Janice realized that he was the one who was to blame for the instability of the marriage, which she had adulterated. She had focused on making him happy. He'd focused on making himself happy.

As she sat on the picturesque beach, she thought about her life again. Now, she was well educated, whereas before she'd been a bumpkin. She'd been provincial and local, but now she had traveled to dozens of cities across the country.

A man came and stood next to her. "Scusa," he smiled.

"Do you speak English?" she asked.

"Yes, I do," he replied. "I'm from Enid, Oklahoma, but I'm bi-lingual. I was hoping you spoke English."

"I'm only fair in Spanish," she admitted, and he grinned.

"May I join you?" he asked.

"Sure," she said, and he spread a towel next to her.

"You're an American also?" he asked.

"Yes, I am," she said. "North Carolina, mostly."

"Married?" he asked. "I'm sorry," he said, noticing her surprised look. "I didn't really want your husband to show up and punch me in the nose. Or ear. Or stomach. Or anywhere else."

"I don't have a husband now," she said. "Divorced. For several years. So the contingency of you getting a punch in the nose seems a bit remote."

"I've never been married," he said.

"Really," she said, a bit of surprise in her voice.

"Thank you," he said. "I'll take that as a compliment."

"You aren't—uh—"

"No, definitely not gay. Just never met the right girl."

"I apologize," she said. "That question was way out of line."

"I'm not offended," he said. "No, I've never had time for marriage."

"What do you do?" she asked.

He told her about his job as a petroleum engineer, and explained that he was on the road most of the year, in Wyoming, Texas, and South America, on occasion to the Middle East Oil States. "So," he said a bit ruefully, "I've made enough money so that I can cut back and not face so much time away from home. I make a good salary, travel to some fun places, get pretty dirty quite a bit, and don't get to meet many Americans. Especially American girls."

"Is that important?" she asked. "That the girls are American?"

"I guess not that important. One of my best friends married a lovely German girl. She's great—fine mother, well-educated, likes to ski and play golf—in addition to being gorgeous. Stan's a happy man, I know."

"You make it sound like it's a problem, though," Janice said.

"The problem is how much traveling he does," said her new friend. "Like me, he's in the plane a lot, overnight out of town up to a week at a time."

"I'm a flight attendant," she said. "I can identify."

"No kids, huh?"

"That's not a happy topic," she said. "I deserted my husband. He got our two daughters in the divorce. Now I never get to see them. In fact, they've made it clear they don't want to see me. That's been pretty hard."

"You sound like you feel guilty about it."

She managed to nod. She didn't really trust herself to speak when the topic of her divorce and her daughters came up.

"Do you have a name?" he asked, after waiting a respectful minute or two.

"I'm Janice O'Neill," she said. "Washington, North Carolina is my home town."

"Blackbeard country," he smiled.

"As a matter of fact, that's right. He had a hideout on the Pamlico Sound."

"My name's Chris Hillman," he said. "I'm from a town in Central Oklahoma. Tornado Alley."

"We fight off hurricanes," she said. "I know the feeling."

The two Americans chatted for several minutes, but Janice yawned and begged leave to take a nap. "Sure," he said. "You got a lot of sunscreen on?"

She didn't, so he reached in his bag for his spray bottle of SPF30. They took turns applying the stuff to one another's backs.

Janice enjoyed herself as he applied the cool lotion to her back. She decided that she'd like to spend the rest of the afternoon with him applying sunscreen to her. She didn't mention this, though.

****

I don't want to run over the mountains again; I want to make a big treaty. I will keep my word until the stones melt; God made the white man and God made the Apache, and the Apache has just as much right to the country as the White Man.

--Chief Delshay of the Tonto Apaches. Brown, p. 192.

Chapter Nineteen

Janice woke up about four o'clock, astounded that she's slept so long. A two-hour nap, she thought. It's been years since I've slept that well in a nap.

She did a quick survey of her body. No sunburn, thank goodness. That was good sunscreen he used, she thought. She glanced around.

He didn't appear to be anywhere nearby, she noticed. That was strange. Oh well, maybe he went to the washroom.

Janice decided to swim in the ocean. Growing up in coastal North Carolina had guaranteed that she had learned to swim about the same time that she learned to walk, and she'd done well in competitive swimming in high school. Her coach had wanted her to go on to swim in college, but she'd had enough of the mind numbing, body draining training. Donning her goggles, she dove into a wave and swam out into the Atlantic Ocean.

The sea was calm and she swam out about 25 yards and turned south, trying not to notice the salt taste of the ocean. She'd gotten used to it as a kid, and been able to tolerate it, but now she wondered how she managed it. Yech!

Janice swam about fifteen minutes south, then turned and swam back. She came out of the ocean and walked to a shower, where she washed the salt away. She walked toward her blanket.

Still no Chris. What the heck? Why would he go without saying goodbye? They'd had a nice conversation, very pleasant and stimulating. But…

Oh, well. Janice picked up her stuff and headed up to her hotel. She showered again, and changed into a short dress she'd purchased at a shop near the hotel, intending to go down for a cocktail and then a dinner in the hotel dining room. Chris still hadn't shown up. She'd managed to avoid sunburn and instead had picked up a nice tan. Too bad, she thought, that Chris wasn't going to see it.

She walked into the living room of her suite and found, to her great surprise, a bouquet of lovely roses sitting on the coffee table. She stood, unable to speak, her mind racing.

She walked forward and picked up the little white card. Nothing except her name and room number.

Janice picked up the room phone. "English?" she asked, when the main desk answered. "Si," said the voice on the other end.

"Main desk?" she said.

"Yes, Madam," said the operator.

"This is Mrs. O'Neill," said Janice, giving her room number. She proceeded to ask about the flower delivery.

The operator put her on hold, and transferred her to the Bell Captain.

"No, Mrs. O'Neill," he said. "We have no information on this delivery. It did not come through us, I assure you."

"How did it get in my room?" asked Janice, and she felt apprehensive and angry at having her room violated.

"I am at a loss," he said. "Let me ask some questions, and I will see what I can find out. I will call you back when I learn something."

Janice told him that would be appreciated and rang off. She went back into the bedroom and put on her makeup and fixed her hair.

She was about to exit the room when the phone rang.

"Mrs. O'Neill?" said the voice.

"Yes."

"I am sorry to disturb you," said the voice. "This is the front desk. A gentleman is here asking to speak with you. May I let him talk to you?"

"Who is it?" she asked.

"Just a moment," said the man. She could hear a muffled conversation. "His name is Christopher Hillman," the bell captain said.

Janice felt deeply spooked by now. She replied, "I will meet him in ten minutes by the front desk."

"Si si," said the man, and hung up.

Ten minutes later, Janice emerged from the elevator and walked toward the front desk.

"My goodness," said Chris, catching sight of her and beaming with approval. He came over to her, his hand outstretched. She took the hand, somewhat wary.

"What can I do for you, Mr. Hillman?" she asked, very formal.

He let go of her hand, backed away a little and frowned. "What's wrong?" he said.

"Oh I don't know," she snapped, more than a trace of sarcasm and accusation in her voice. "Why don't we start with, 'where did you go on the beach?'"

"I received a phone call and had to go into the city," he said, mystified. "I told you I'd call for you this evening. Here I am."

"I thought you'd taken off," she said.

"Why would you think that?" he asked. "I told you where I was going. You agreed and said I should call for you here at

7:00. That's the time, this is the place."

Janice went cold. She had no memory of such a conversation. "I see," she said, "but I don't recall anything of such an agreement. Certainly not an invitation to dinner."

His face changed now. "Okay," he said. "I guess I misunderstood when you said that was fine."

"I probably would have said that," she said, "if you'd said it."

He stood agape, an expression of absolute bewilderment on his face.

"Janice," he began, but she cut him off, realizing that she must have sounded strange to this man.

"I'm sorry," she responded, "Something strange is going on. I would love to have dinner with you, if you still want to."

The two-people stood, staring in one another's eyes. Could this have happened? Why don't I remember this? Janice asked herself, trying not to show her bewilderment.

A few moments later, their cab dropped them at a fine Brazilian restaurant, Adega Perola, not far from the Copacabana hotel where Janice was staying. Two Brazilian themed cocktails called Cuiprinhas introduced them to the food of one of the top ten restaurants in Rio.

Janice sipped her cocktail and looked across at her tablemate. She saw not the slightest hint of duplicity in his demeanor or his eyes. What could have happened? She asked herself. She liked this man, and didn't know how she could have forgotten an invitation to dinner.

Chris said, after an awkward pause, "Okay. Can we talk about this?"

Janice hesitated, and then said, "Sure."

"Look, I'd like to continue to get to know you," he said. "I don't want something like a misunderstanding to come between us."

"Okay," she said, and added softly, "I don't either."

"Janice," he said. "Do you really not remember me asking you to dinner?"

"I've been wracking my brain about it," she said. "I remember you spraying my back with sunscreen. Then I made a pillow out of a towel, said I was going to sleep, and I woke up two hours later."

"But we continued talking for quite a while before you fell asleep," he said.

Their appetizers arrived and they made small talk for a few moments. Then, she asked, "Did you send me roses?"

He paused with his fork halfway to his mouth. "Send you roses?" he repeated.

"Yes," she said. "I came out of the shower and found them on the dresser. A nice vase, a neutral note—"

"What did the note say?"

"Nothing," she said. "Just my name and room number."

"Did you call the bell captain?" he asked.

"Sure," she said. "He was asking around, to see if any of the bellmen let someone into my room. He hadn't called me back as of the time we left."

"Did you set the security lock?" he asked.

She thought. "Yes, I think so."

"So, no one could have gotten in."

"No, it seems..." Now she broke off. "Wait a second. That means..."

"Yes, I think it does," he said. "Someone was in your room when you came from the beach, wasn't he?"

She hesitated, thinking it over. Then, she said, "You're telling me it wasn't you."

"No," he said. "It couldn't have been. I had an hour meeting in town with an officer from the Oil Company I'm consulting with. I went back to my room after the guy called me on the beach. I grabbed a quick shower and headed over to the meeting in a cab. I got back about twenty minutes before I headed down and called your room."

Janice sat in silence. "I think I want to get out of here," she said. "Away from Brazil."

"Now?" he asked.

"Yes, now," she said. "Tonight."

Their dinners arrived. Janice managed to eat some of the astounding beef and some of the seafood, but she was scared.

"Look," said Chris. "Let's get a jet out of here. My business is done. I can grab my luggage and we can head back to the states."

Janice stared blankly. "Sure," she mumbled.

"Are you sure you want me to come with you? Is that okay?"

She squeezed his hand in appreciation. "Not okay," she said. "That would be wonderful." As she said this, she realized that she implicitly trusted this man. Now that she was with him again, she didn't and couldn't believe for an instant that he was duplicitous.

Chris called the hotel and asked security to check her room, and then his, and to have their bills ready. He found a flight to Miami and booked two seats. An hour later, they were back at their hotel.

Chris accompanied Janice to her room. She packed and was ready to go in moments. She closed up her room and walked with Chris to his, some ten floors below. She waited while he packed, and then walked with him to the elevator.

They crossed the lobby to a waiting cab and drove off. "Can you make sure we aren't being followed?" he asked the driver, speaking excellent Portuguese. The driver looked a little bewildered at first. Still, he drove a route to the airport that would have been hard for an eagle to follow. Chris tipped him well and received a handshake.

At midnight, they boarded a night coach, relatively certain they hadn't been followed. "Thank you," Janice said. "I appreciate what you've done for me."

"What did I do?" he asked. "I had to come back to the states too. We just moved everything up a little."

"You kept me from being scared," she said. "It's the first time in a little while."

He took the aisle seat. The attendants gave them each a pillow and a blanket. She leaned against him as they fell asleep.

*****

They woke, both feeling that they could have slept for another 6 hours, as the plane landed about 7:30 A. M. "Gack," said Janice. "I've never slept so well."

"Yeah," said the man next to her. "I feel a bit cheated though. I should have had sex before I went to sleep."

Janice giggled and whacked his arm. He suggested a bite of breakfast at the airport and they found a grille in the airport that served them eggs and bacon.

"What do we do now?" he asked.

"I don't know," she shrugged. "Rio was wonderful. It's good to be back in the U. S., though."

"Shall we head up to Raleigh-Durham? Then Chapel Hill?"

"I think I should," she said. "But what about you? Don't you have work to do?"

He shrugged. "Do you have an internet hook-up in Chapel Hill?"

"Sure," she said. "But we won't be back there for several hours, right?"

"Doesn't matter," he said. "As long as you feel safe."

"I think I am," she said. "When I'm with you, I feel safe."

"Thank you," he grinned.

They found a flight to Raleigh-Durham, but they had what seemed like an infinite walk to the gate where Janice was again drafted to help serve the flight. It was okay, she thought, because she didn't have to fly alone.

*****

Why is it that the Apaches want to die—that they carry their lives on their fingernails? They roamed over the hills and plains and want the heavens to fall on them. The Apaches were once a great nation; they are but few, and because of this they want to die and carry their lives on their fingernails.

--Chief Cochise of the Chiricahua Apaches. Brown, p. 192.

Chapter Twenty

The flight touched down at noon at Raleigh-Durham, and they took a cab to her apartment. Janice picked up her car and took the opportunity to share with Chris all the strange things that had been going on, then drove them to Chapel Hill. The campus of the University of North Carolina made quite an impression on him.

"Well, I'm impressed." he said as she showed him around the campus. "What a beautiful school."

"I know," she said, not without a little pride in showing off her Alma Mater. "Look, let me have your opinion. Do you think we could have fallen on our feet here? Could we be safe?"

"It appears that way," he admitted. "Still, look at the last few hours. Someone seems to have the ability to track you, don't you agree?"

She considered. "Okay, then they must know we're—or at least I'm—here."

He looked thoughtful for a few moments. "Did you say you knew a cop here in town?"

"Not well," she admitted. "But he knows who I am. Why?"

"How about you call him?"

Janice hesitated, but then extracted her cell phone from her purse and speed dialed Jim's number. "Detective Kruger speaking," he said.

"Jim, this is Janice O'Neill."

"Yes, Janice," he said. "Glad you called. Are you okay?"

"Well, I guess so," she said. "Is there a way I could meet with you?"

"Sure," he said. "Where?"

"I think I'll come in to the station," she said. "Can you direct me?" He gave her directions and twenty minutes later she walked into the station. Jim and Chris shook hands, and the cop took them to an interview room. Janice brought the detective up to date.

"Let me make sure I understand," he said. "You've spent the last few days in Rio de Janeiro and someone stalked you there?"

"That's what I'm telling you, yes," she acknowledged. "Here's the card from the florist. I don't know how they got in my room."

"The card came with the flowers, right?"

"Yes, but the florist in Rio told me that he never saw the man who bought them," she explained. "Some peasant boy brought in the order. That's the way it's been done here, too."

"Right. I've spent some time trying to trace anything I could from the cards, but each one has been a dead end. The guy has covered his tracks. Are you telling me that no one from the hotel put those flowers in your room?"

"That's exactly what I'm telling you," confirmed Janice.

"Is there anything you can do to him if you catch him?" asked Chris.

Jim looked at Chris. "I don't know," he said. "That's a good question. He hasn't hurt you, has he, Janice?"

"Unless you count scaring me," she said.

"That's significant, Detective," said Chris. "I know how nervous and worried she's been. She's even traveled internationally to get away from whoever this is."

"She's lucky to have you helping her," acknowledged Jim. "The expense also must be incredible for both of you."

"I get a break from the airline, of course," said Janice.

"I'm traveling on my company's dime," added Chris. "I'm managing to get some work done on my computer with e-mail. I appreciate your concern, though."

"I promise I'll keep working on this thing," said Jim the cop. "I'm not having much luck. Whoever did this planned and executed it well."

Janice leaned back. She bit at a nail for a few moments while Chris took her hand and stroked the palm with his thumb. "It's going to be okay," he assured her. "We'll get it going."

"Who's doing this?" she blurted. "Why? What on earth does he want with me?"

Chris smiled at her. "You are pretty attractive, you know."

Janice gave him a quizzical look but then asked, "You mean you think its physical attraction?"

"That's my first reaction too," said Jim the cop. "It sounds like you've become his hobby."

"What can I do about it?" Janice pleaded.

"Have you given any more thought to re-locating, at least for a while?" asked Jim.

"Now look heyah," drawled Chris, "I live in Oklahoma. Pretty nice place. Want me to sing 'Oklahoma Hills' for you?" He cleared his throat. "'Many years have come and gone since Ah wandered from mah home, In the Oklahoma hills where Ah was bawn—'"

"Okay," she said. "I've got the picture."

"Just a minute," he said, "I'm coming to the best part: 'Way down yonder on the Indian Nation a cowboy's life is mah occupation—"

Janice waved her arms to stop the concert. When he was

silent, she stared at her friend for several moments. "Woody Guthrie. Second World War, about. His son Arlo has a good version on You Tube," he added, trying to be helpful.

"Do you have a place you could stay for a few weeks, until we get this sorted out?" Jim asked, who had been chuckling at the Country music concert.

"That's why I sang "Oklahoma Hills," said Chris, grinning.

"Chris," she said. "Are you asking me to live with you?"

"Well, maybe," he said. "That would be up to you. We can get you a room in town if you want, or set up an apartment at my house, or…" He didn't finish the sentence since she poked him in the rib. "Anyhow, Enid is a pretty nice town."

"But we just met a few days ago," she said.

"I know," he said. "Think about it. Meanwhile, we have to make sure you're not being followed or tracked anymore."

"I can help there," said Jim. "Let me have your stuff scanned for bugs."

He left the room, and Janice took the opportunity to call Gus at the gas station and tell him what was going on. Gus told her not to worry and take care of things. "I'm sure glad you called. I was beginning to get worried since I hadn't heard from you for a few days."

A half hour later, Jim came back to the office and handed Janice her purse. "We found a tracker," he said. "I'm having my guys try to run it down. We could put this thing in a dummy suitcase and send it to Outer Slobbovia, too."

"Are you kidding me?" Janice gasped. "Someone planted a bug in my purse?"

"Yeah," replied Jim.

"Let's send it as far away as possible," agreed Janice. "Just get rid of the things, whatever they are."

Jim wished her luck, and after several more minutes, Janice and Chris left the police station and took a jet to New York. They had their cab driver take her to the International terminal at Kennedy International.

Janice took her newly purchased gym bag to luggage check-in for Peru, and after paying a nominal fee, waved good-bye to the little grip containing the tracker bug and accompanied Chris back into the American Airline terminal. They boarded a jet, which would take them to Dallas. From there they would rent a car and drive to Enid, Oklahoma.

"Do you think we're safe now?" asked Janice as they sat on the runway waiting for the jet to take them to Dallas. It was a night coach and Janice had waited for the last person to board before they went in to find their seats.

"You saw no one who looked familiar, right?" Chris asked.

"Right," she said.

"Okay," he said. "Try and get some sleep."

She leaned against his shoulder and for a while, at least, everything felt okay.

*****

If the Texans had kept out of my country there might have been peace. But that which you say we must live on is too small. The Texans have taken away the places where the grass grew the thickest and the timber was the best. Had we kept that, we might have done the things you asked. But now it is too late. The white man has the country, which we loved and we only wish to wander on the prairie until we die.

--Parba Wa-Samen (Chief Ten Bears) of the Yamparika Comanches. Brown, p, 242.

CHAPTER TWENTY-ONE

The flight landed late in the morning. Janice rented a car and they drove to Enid, about a five-hour drive. They had a quick dinner, and began to get ready for bed.

"Do you mind…" she began, not sure how to broach the subject. "Is it okay…"?

"What," he drawled, grinning at her.

"Do you mind a lot if we don't sleep together?"

He laughed out loud. "Of course, I mind," he said. "But I'd rather not put you in any uncomfortable situation where you have to make some sort of a decision you're not ready to make. You can let me know, okay?"

He went to his bedroom, but Janice had a hard time relaxing. She felt so comfortable around this man, as if she'd known him for years. He'd been so kind, thoughtful, and understanding—

And a little bell went off in her mind. Why?

She considered. Men had always found her attractive and she used her wiles to enhance their feelings. That was why she'd had affairs: she liked the flattery, the knowledge that another person found her attractive.

She'd been involved with a very nice man for about a year at one point. He was a family man, with a good job, beautiful home, and a classic car that he cared for as if it was one of his kids. She went along with the affair for several months because she found him attractive, a considerate lover and—

Well, she'd liked the adventure. She knew it was wrong, that it went against all she'd been taught and even believed and had, until that year, been scrupulous in observing—

And certainly, she'd never pursued anything permanent.

She'd finally ended it when she decided that she had to see what his intentions were. He was surprised, she thought. He'd been happy with the arrangement, and enjoyed the sneaking, the hiding, and the getting away for an occasional weekend or even just over night.

She had a hard time breaking it off. She missed him, or, to be more accurate, she'd missed the lovemaking. But she couldn't, she knew, let it continue. Her husband had been distant, even difficult during the few years leading up to the affair, and even after it.

A year or two passed before she had another sexual relation. Then she had several in a row, one-night stands, an occasional weekend away.

And then, the moment came when she realized that she didn't love, didn't respect, and didn't want to be with her husband. Setting up the escape had been far from guilt free, but she had set it up with precision.

And then her intended had dumped her, taking off for the west coast.

She sat in her bed, arms wrapped around her legs. What should she do now? Should she commit to this wonderful man named Chris? Or should she see how things would go?

Abruptly, she knew that she couldn't continue without his input. She was sorry to wake him—well, somewhat sorry—but she had to talk to him at that moment.

She stood and walked down the hall to his room. His door was shut, but she could see a little slip of light between the door and the carpet. She tapped on the door.

"Come in," his voice boomed. "I've been expecting you."

She opened the door, and found him sitting on top of his covers, wearing a sweat suit.

"Hi," she said. "Do you always wear a sweat suit to bed?"

"Only when I'm expecting visitors. Sometimes I'll wear a business suit with a white shirt and tie, but only for formal sleeps."

She laughed a little. "You took that from Neil Simon."

"Yeah," he confessed. "Barefoot in the Park, to be specific."

"Do you like theatre?" she asked.

"Sure," he said. "Movies, too. An occasional TV show, but not often."

"Me too," she agreed. He drew back the blanket on her side. She hesitated for a second, but then she slid in, propping a pillow behind her and sitting against the headboard.

They talked for nearly two hours. They spent the time exploring memories, childhood and college experiences, the difference between growing up in Oklahoma and North Carolina.

Near three o'clock in the morning, she mumbled, "I'm sorry. I'm having trouble keeping my eyes open."

"I'm not surprised," he said. "I have that effect on women." He gave an elaborate sigh.

She giggled. "Martyrdom does become you," she said. Then she hesitated. "Can…" She hesitated again.

He waited with patience, though tapping his finger on the bedside table.

At last: "Can I stay here?"

"Sure," he said, and turned out the bedside light.

*****

Janice woke up and looked over at the man next to her. He

hadn't even touched her. He'd honored his promise, despite having her in his bed. She'd slept well, and she realized that she truly trusted this man.

Was the time right? She wondered. She decided that no, it wasn't. She had to learn more about him, what he did, what his ideas and goals were, his religious views, his politics, and did he want something new-- like her -- in his life. Where would they live?

That last: She'd lived in North Carolina almost all her life. She loved the ocean, the beach, the seafood, the history of the area and coastal life in general.

But she had no one, now. Really, she didn't. Her parents had died. Her cousins had moved away. Her ex-husband had re-married and she'd blown it with her two daughters, who never wanted to see her again.

Can a person start her life over again? She considered. She thought about the Christian—what would you call it? A motto? A mantra? —That "You must be born again."

What did that mean? She asked herself. Someone had asked Jesus if that meant you had to re-enter your mother's womb. He had denied that idea.

She thought about the Angel Curiel. He'd assured her that she'd entered into a salvation Covenant with Christ years ago. If that was true—and she could think of no reason that her Angel friend would lie to her—then was she still under that promise? Did she belong to Him but didn't realize it?

She chopped a few potatoes, an onion, and a green pepper. She found a frying pan, poured in a little vegetable oil and began to saute the potatoes.

While they fried, she resumed her thoughts.

This stalker had scared her badly, and why? She didn't know that he was dangerous, though the idea of having someone monitoring all of her movements frightened her all the time.

For one thing, she couldn't bring up any idea of who he was. What did he want? Okay, she did have money. She'd invested her money wisely and had a good retirement fund developing, a few stocks, some bonds and a fair money market. But there were lots of women who had a lot more money than she, of course.

Sex?

Surely not. She'd had some affairs, yes, but they hadn't been public knowledge. She'd been careful not to discuss them with anybody. Unless the men had blabbed about the affairs, but as she ticked them off, they wouldn't have wanted anyone to know about it. Sure.

Well, she couldn't rule it out, but it seemed unlikely.

She dropped some bacon into another pan as the potatoes neared completion, and then put in some toast. The coffee had brewed and she poured herself a cup.

She drank it in small sips to make the savor last. She buttered the toast and set it on a plate, then scrambled eight eggs. She mixed in some cheese, and in a few moments scooped the eggs onto the plate.

Then she poured another cup of coffee and walked down the hall to his bedroom. She knocked and came in as he awoke. She took the coffee over to him and waved a hand over the top as his eyes came open.

"Out of the sack," she commanded. "Breakfast is served in the kitchen." He grabbed the coffee, took a large slurp, then stood and slipped into the bathrobe she held up for him.

Five minutes later, they were well on the way to devouring everything in sight. He raved about the breakfast and especially the coffee.

"I'm the world's worst at coffee," he said, giving her a rueful grin. "What time is it?"

She looked at her watch. "Five to eight," she said. "The key is to put just a slight pinch of salt in the grounds as it is brewing."

"How do you feel about going to my church this morning?" he asked. "We have a service at 9:15."

Oh, right, she thought. It's Sunday. "Well," she said. "I don't have a church at home, but I'd like to start."

"Okay," he said. "We're pretty casual, so don't go to a lot of trouble. Can you be ready in about 40 minutes?" She agreed that she could.

She went into the guest bedroom, slipped into a robe, and entered the bathroom to take her shower. While she was busy getting dressed, Chris cleaned up the kitchen, put the food away, and changed into a sport shirt and a pair of khakis. As promised, they were on the road I plenty of time to make the service.

*****

The Comanches had developed an agricultural economy in Texas, but the white man had come there and seized their farmlands, forcing them to hunt buffalo in order to survive. Now this kindly old man, Bald Head Tatum was trying to tell them they should take the white man's road and go to farming, as if the Indians knew nothing of growing corn. Was it not the Indian who taught the white man how to plant corn and make it grow?

Chapter Twenty-Two

The church was a large one, with a congregation in the hundreds. Several people greeted her, and made her feel welcome. The singing was professional and well-rehearsed, and the pastor's sermon spoke well to her. At several points, she felt herself convicted of her life and knew that she had some things she still needed to work through.

After the service, Chris introduced her to several of his friends who extended a gracious welcome to her with kindness and affection. It was clear that the people liked and valued Chris. She learned that he served on a few committees and worked with the treasurer of the church.

Good grief, she thought. What have I fallen into?

*****

After the service, Chris suggested that they stay for a Bible Study and then a church picnic. Janice, touched that they had been invited, asked if they could bring something. "Funny you should ask," he said. "I have a watermelon in the trunk. Will that be okay?"

The picnic featured ham and cheese sandwiches, barbecued beef and pork, potato salad and green salads, along with all the traditional potluck side dishes and desserts that the people of the congregation had supplied. Janice enjoyed lemonade and thought about how nice it would be to stay and talk for the rest of the afternoon and evening, spending time making friends with these good solid people.

The picnic continued into the early evening when Janice and

Chris volunteered to help with cleanup. The moon was full as they drove to Chris' house. Janice, dead-tired, struggled to keep her eyes open as they turned onto Chris' street.

"Huh," he said. "Whose car is that?" He pointed at a nondescript sedan that sat in front of his house.

"Don't you know?" she asked.

"Nope," he said. He used the garage door opener and pulled in. He told her to stay in the car until the door had lowered all the way down. They went into the house, but Chris said, "Stay out of sight."

He sneaked out the back door and crept up on the car. Janice saw that he had a pistol in his hand, which he had apparently grabbed in the utility room before he exited. She saw the driver's window lower, and she opened the front door so she could hear what was happening.

"Who are you?" asked Chris, speaking to the person inside.

"What's it to you?" asked the person inside. She could hear the sneer in the man's voice.

"Okay," insisted Chris. "Beat it before I call the cops."

The driver's right hand came up and she could see a pistol in the man's hand. Chris's right hand shot out and shoved the hand forward, smashing the wrist against the window track in the door. The gun discharged into a tree and fell to the ground.

A second or two later she heard the first scream of agony as the pain of a compound fracture of the wrist hit the driver with full force. "Janice," yelled Chris, putting his pistol in the man's left ear.

Janice ran to the scene, high heels clicking on the sidewalk and driveway. "Call the police," shouted Chris. He sounded remarkably calm.

The Enid police joined the scene in a few minutes and dragged the whimpering thug out of his car. They put the man into their cruiser. "We better get this guy to a hospital," they said.

"Any idea who he is?" asked one of the cops.

"I've never seen him before," said Chris.

"Me neither," said Janice.

"Any idea why he pulled a gun on you?" asked the other cop.

"I asked him who he was and what he wanted," answered Chris. "I guess that he wanted to intimidate me."

"I think he was after me," said Janice.

The two cops turned to her. "Why?" the first cop asked.

"I think he's hired muscle," she explained. "I've had a stalker chasing me for several months. Yes, you can confirm with the Police in Washington, North Carolina. I think the stalker paid the thug to find me and bring me to him."

She told briefly the story of the man, the gas station, and the subsequent harassment she'd dealt with.

At last the police bid them good night and told them they'd be in touch.

Janice and Chris went back in the house. When the door shut, she put her arms around him and wept for a long time.

*****

The next morning, they sat across from each other at the breakfast table, sipping coffee. They'd spent quite a bit of time talking and sharing their lives with one another while cuddling on the sofa in some romantic candlelight. She still didn't want to complicate the relationship by becoming intimate. Again he'd been wonderful, calm and not demanding. Janice, however, was still upset about the attack the night before.

She wrapped her hands around her cup. To her embarrassment, she began to cry. She apologized. "Chris, is this ever going to end?" Janice asked when she at last gained a little control.

"I don't have a clue," he said. "I can't imagine someone going to the point of hiring people to chase down an unrequited love."

"I wonder if this could be a guy from Chapel Hill. I had trouble with him while I was working at Gus' station," she said, "He couldn't be in love with me. I haven't exchanged a hundred words with him in my life. But if it is him, suddenly a lot of things make sense. He must want something, but I can't imagine why he'd go to this much trouble."

"Tell me what you know," he said.

She told him how she'd whacked the man with her fist wrapped around the deep socket from her tool kit.. "He grabbed me," she explained. "So I hit him in the Adam's Apple. Police have told me that he has a rasp in his voice to this day."

He thought about that for a moment. "I see. So in return he blames you, huh?"

"That's all I can assume," she said. "I've never been stalked before. Maybe the idea is just to frighten me."

He frowned. "He's gone to a lot of trouble, hasn't he? For a punch in the throat? To say nothing of a pile of money that he's expended."

She thought about that. "Well, I don't know," she said. "As you can imagine, I've tried to think about any other explanation, but it continues to elude me."

"So, you figure he'll continue to come after you?" he asked.

"That's what the evidence suggests," she asserted. Chris left a few moments after this conversation to take a shower.

Janice decided that she needed to de-stress a little. She walked over to the bathroom door and yelled in to Chris, "I'm going out for a run. I'll be back in a little while." Exercise had always helped, so she changed into some sweat clothes and took a lengthy run through the neighborhood, enjoying the sweat and the muscle ache. Meanwhile, she let herself think about the last few days, working her way through the situation into which she'd fallen.

As she ran, she tried again to figure why a man would go to such trouble to harm her. Could it be that he just wanted to frighten her? So far she really hadn't been harmed.

But she began to focus her thoughts. Her reaction to the stalking again and again had been to flee: Rio; Nashville; Oklahoma and so forth. Why hadn't she confronted the man? Get him into a room and question him: ask him what he wanted, tell him she couldn't muster any interest in him, wanted nothing to do with him…

And then it struck her.

What if this wasn't a stalking for the sake of romance?

She stopped in a park, found a fountain and took a long drink of water. She walked around for a few moments, trying to clear her head.

She didn't consider herself a ravishing beauty. She was tall, and had a good, though not a staggering figure. Yes, she was well educated now and articulate, but she wasn't that way when this thing started. She had been just plain Janice, uneducated, unprincipled, immoral and with nothing particular to offer.

Why would someone stalk her?

Janice's parents had been dead since she was a young girl.

Her maternal grandfather and grandmother had adopted her and they had been warm and loving as parents. Her parents had deserted her—not by choice, to be sure, but the effect was the same—and she'd never been close to her father's parents. They had lived too far away except for an occasional visit

In school, she'd had very few friends. She'd become rebellious, feeling resentful and defensive about her Native American heritage which seemed to set her apart from all the other kids at her school.

The biggest surprise of her life came when she'd just finished her master's degree. Her maternal grandparents had contacted her and told her that she she had reached the age where they could finally divulge the details of her inheritance.

Her parents' estate had been substantial, and her father's parents were naming her the principal beneficiary of their estate as well. When she reached the age of thirty, she inherited a great deal of money, stocks and bonds, and real estate.

She was past that age now, and hadn't still had not settled her estate. She'd been trying to get her life going—-

And now she'd met Chris. She could see herself building a life around this fine man. Was she being hasty?

Perhaps, but she didn't think so.

Wait a moment. There was the folder that contained all the wills, the personal papers, and the non-material possessions of her parents and her grandparents.

She had to go back to North Carolina, now. Well, in a day or two. She had to fly tomorrow, and she planned to fly from Enid to Chicago. Then from Chicago she'd hop to New York, then to Los Angeles, then back again. She decided she'd take a hop over to Atlanta and then to Raleigh and drive home. She'd jump back on the shuttle and make her way back to Enid with the inheritance folder.

Good grief, she thought. I won't get in till late. Maybe I should be cautious.

I forgot, she said, that I've got Chris. I wonder if he could come with me?

Janice turned back to her run and got back to the house in a much shorter time than it taken her to get out.

And then, it occurred to her.

It was the money. Somehow, the thug who was chasing her knew that she had a great deal of money. If the stalker killed her, he was planning to contrive a way that he could get at her money, her investments. That had to be it.

He planned to rob her and kill her. Then, he'd steal the money.

*****

Even Kicking Bird was offended by the governor's demands: "My heart is as stone; there is no soft spot in it. I have taken the white man by the hand, thinking him to be a friend; but he is not a friend. Government has deceived us. Washington is rotten."

--Kicking Bird of the Kiowas. Brown, p. 262.

CHAPTER TWENTY-THREE

Chris was napping, while the TV was turned to a Sunday afternoon ballgame. She walked over to his lounge chair.

He sensed her presence and woke up.

"Hey," he said. "Have a nice run?"

"Yes," she said. "Do you like children?"

He chuckled. "Of course, I do. I—"

"Have you ever been in trouble with the police or the law in general?"

"Well," he shrugged. "I did knife a guy in a Tijuana bar fight a couple of summers ago. A few years before that I hijacked a plane headed to Quantico and flew it to Cuba. Before that, I…"

"I'm serious," she interrupted.

He stared at her. "What do you mean?"

"This is the big question," she asked. "Do you think you can learn to love me and stay with me from now on?"

He hesitated. "Is that where this is going? A promise of marriage?"

"Not exactly," she said. "I don't want a marriage that will last for a year, or two years, or ten. I want to marry you for the rest of our lives. I want to have kids with you. I want to live here and go to the church and PTA."

"Isn't this a little sudden?"

"Yes," she said. "It's very sudden. What's your answer?"

"Do you have to know this minute or can I think about it for a little bit?"

"This minute," she said.

He swallowed. "Well, I'll tell you," he said. Then he stood

up, took her in his arms and gave her the most profound kiss she'd ever experienced.

A half hour later, he came back into the room, having spent several minutes on the phone with the church's pastor. "Okay," he said. "Pastor isn't crazy about the idea. Oh he'll do it," he assured her. "He said if we were a couple of kids he'd never go for it. But since we're adults, and clearly love each other, he can do it as soon as we want."

"How about right now?" she asked.

"Look, what's the rush?" he rejoined.

"I'll tell you," she said, "but not until we're married."

*****

Janice went to a local mall, where she purchased a stylish pale apricot colored dress and a new pair of heels. By the time she returned, Chris had changed into a formal suit, and before she knew it, they were two minutes out from the church.

"Chris," she mumbled.

"Hmm?" he said, watching the road.

"You don't have to do this," she said. "I'm sorry I pushed you this hard."

"Are you backing out?"

"No, not me," she said. "I want to go through with this."

"Okay, then so do I," Chris grinned.

Then they pulled into the church parking lot. Pastor Cliff and his wife were waiting, and a group of Chris' friends, including Charley, his lifetime best friend, who would serve as his best man.

"Ready?" said Cliff.

"Yes," Janice and Chris said.

"Simple ceremony?" he asked.

"As possible," she agreed.

Twenty minutes later they left the church after accepting congratulations from all in attendance. Chris gave the keys to his car to Pastor Cliff, who promised to drive it home and park it in the garage.

An hour later, they were on a shuttle to Atlanta. Three hours later, they landed in Chicago. They were just in time to catch a flight to Augusta, Maine, and were in the air in less than twenty minutes.

"This worked out pretty well," said Chris.

"Yes," she said. "It couldn't have worked better."

****

The great leaders were gone; the mighty power of the Kiowas and the Comanches was broken; the buffalo they had tried to save had vanished. It had all happened in ten years.

--Brown, p. 271.

CHAPTER TWENTY-FOUR

The plane was only half full, fortunately, and she turned to talk with him.

"Okay," he said. "What is this? What is the big hurry?"

"I didn't want you to feel that you'd married me for my money," Janice told him. "Not too long ago I discovered I have inherited a great deal of money—"

"You have?" he asked, and she could see that the statement had taken him aback.

"Yes," she said. "It turns out, though, that we may become very wealthy."

"Slow down, Janice. What are you talking about?" he asked, when he could talk again.

She explained about her inheritance. Yes, she was the only heir, had no brothers or sisters, and her parents were gone. Except for him, she had no living relatives, except for an elderly grandmother and grandfather.

"That's why I wanted to get married right away, " she said. "Would you be okay if we started a family as soon as we can? You know I am not getting any younger."

"Jan," he said, using the diminutive of her name. "Please believe me. I really and truly had no such knowledge of your past when we got married."

She took his arm and snuggled against him. "I believe you," she said. "I don't think you're capable of deceit."

"Thanks," he smiled.

"As I've considered it," she said, "I think that's why the guy is after me."

"But…" he began. "How could he know…I mean, how could he get his mitts on your money anyway?" She shook her head.

"I don't know," she said. "But suddenly I just know that's what's involved. I want to get the money invested and safe from him. He wants to destroy me, not just kill me."

After landing in Maine, Janice spent a good deal of time on the phone before dinner. She was pretty secretive about her conversations.

They spent their wedding night in a nice hotel in Boothbay Harbor where she had come years before with her parents. The sex had been worth waiting for: they were slow, deliberate, relishing one another. From the first, she'd laid back, just embracing him, enjoying him, not violent but warm and gentle. In the morning, they lounged for some time, talking, relaxing,

"So," said Janice, "you really are a clean Gene, huh?"

He laughed at the awkward nickname. "Oh, I didn't tell you everything."

"Like what?"

"Well, I play golf at a local club. The seventeenth has a huge sand trap in the rough shape of Mickey Mouse." She snorted behind her hand. "One time, I had a chance to break 80 for the first time. Then, I hit my second shot right into the middle of this trap. I got stuck in there and took eight strokes to get out. Then I was so outraged that I didn't rake the trap. Oh, no! You draw back! You are horrified!"

"I'm not horrified," she said. "I'm laughing at you."

They continued the teasing and joking for some time, but at about 10:00 A. M., however, Janice told him to shower and change for the day. She had already arranged a schedule for them. They left the room just before eleven and she took his hand. They rode the elevator to the top floor.

Janice walked down the corridor to a room near the end of the hall and knocked on the door. A man opened the door and admitted them.

"Chris," she announced, "this is a friend of mine, Bob Lambert, and his wife Amy. They're going to become us."

"What? Why?" asked Chris, surprised by this announcement.

"I think we've been followed," she said. "I suspected that someone was watching us as we boarded the plane to come out here. Bob and Amy are going to switch places with us for a couple of days."

"What?" mumbled Chris again.

"They're going to take our rental car and head north," she explained. "I'm hoping they look enough like us to lead our little tail feathers away while we go south."

"So…"

"They're going to take our car and go to Mount Desert Island," said Janice, proud of her little plan.

"Why?" asked Chris.

"Because that's where they keep Bar Harbor," said Janice.

"Oh," said Chris, poking her in the ribs.

An hour later, Chris and Janice drove south in the car rented by Bob and Amy, while Janice's friends headed north in the car Chris had rented. Chris headed west out of Boothbay to the I-95 Interstate and then to the airport in Portland. They returned the rental car and hopped on the shuttle to the main terminal.

Once they arrived at the terminal Janice met a man named Alan Smith whom she introduced to her new husband. "Al is an old friend. We went to high school together. He lives near

Augusta, not far from the ocean." Chris and Al shook hands, and Chris thanked him for helping them out.

"Is the plane ready?" she asked him.

"Yes ma'am," grinned Alan. He led them to a car and drove them to a private hangar where a Lear Jet awaited them. In ten minutes they were again in the air, headed south.

"Where are we going this time?" asked Chris, becoming amused at all the cloak and dagger antics.

"Raleigh," said Janice. "Then we're going to drive a bit."

"How far?"

"About 2 hours, maybe a bit more," shrugged Janice. "Back to Washington. You'll love the Pamlico Sound at this time of year."

"We're going to rent another car?"

"Yep," said Janice. "It's waiting for us."

"How did you manage to set this thing up?" he said, in an awkward voice.

"I know some people from working in the airline business that I can call when I need help," she said. "I've been setting it up as we travel. I'm trying to keep our whereabouts as quiet as possible."

"Look, Honey—" he began.

"Don't you 'Honey' me, Buster," she returned with an indignant sniff.

They giggled. "What can I call you?" he laughed. "I need a pet name."

She thought. "Here's a wild idea. How about Janice?"

"No, I mean as a term of endearment," he persisted. "You know, like a little nickname?"

"I don't know," she said. "My cousin Tim used to call his wife 'Pumpkey', sort of a variant on Pumpkin, you see."

"You want me to call you that?"

"Well, if you do," she said, "just sleep with one eye open, because I may hit you with a tomahawk."

"Yow," he said. "So we can rule out 'Pumpkey.' "

"Absolutely correct," said Janice. "Consider that a warning."

"Right," he said.

"Now, that's not bad," she replied with approval.

"What's not bad?" he asked.

"'Right'," she said. "Just keep telling people I'm 'Right'."

"Good one," he said.

"It'd save a lot of trouble," she shrugged.

*****

"We want no white men here. The Black Hills belong to me. If the whites try to take them, I will fight." Tatanka Yotanka (Sitting Bull)

"One does not sell the earth upon which the people walk." Tashunka Witko (Chief Crazy Horse)

--Brown, p. 233

CHAPTER TWENTY-FIVE

The jet landed at a private runway at Raleigh, and Janice and Chris hustled to the rental car agency. Janice chose a nondescript sedan and they set off. They pulled into Washington, North Carolina, and Janice directed him to a restaurant called Bank Bistro and Bar.

The waitress took their cocktail orders and advised them that she couldn't tell them the evening special. "Why not?" asked Janice.

"A guy was fishing off the pier here in town about an hour ago and caught a nice mackerel," the waitress said. "He brought it in to us. I can't tell you because the chef is still deciding what he wants to do with it. So if you—"

"We'll have it," said Chris and Janice in unison. The waitress laughed and noted their choice.

Janice had a dirty martini and Chris stayed with soda. "You don't drink much, do you?" she observed.

"I prefer the real stuff," he said.

"You mean Moonshine?" she giggled.

"You might call it that," he said. "Back in Okie Country, it's real if it's homemade, rather than that store-bought sludge."

"This is Beefeater's Gin!" she said, with more than a touch of reproach in her voice.

"Well, as store-bought goes, it doesn't get any better," he agreed. "But you'll have to try some of my grandpa's real gin."

"Does it double as paint remover?" she asked.

"Probably could," he admitted. "Two drinks and you notice that you can't make a fist."

"Does he make it in a bathtub?" she smiled.

"No, don't be silly," he scoffed. "He uses the utility sink in the basement." Janice laughed, and he joined her. The teasing and laughing continued and felt so good that they barely noticed when their meals showed up.

The dish turned out to be pesto pasta with the seared mackerel served on top and covered in pesto sauce. Janice took two bites and announced that she couldn't remember a better meal in her hometown.

Chris agreed with her evaluation, and with her selection of a maple cheesecake for dessert. They enjoyed the maple syrup drizzled over the cheesecake and sat relaxing with a cup of coffee.

Toward the end of the meal, a man in a casual short sleeve shirt approached the table and greeted Janice.

"Hello, Tony," she said. "Chris, say hi to my attorney, Tony DeLuca. I called him, too."

The two men sat down and engaged in some chitchat until Janice suggested they discuss some business over coffee. Tony nodded.

"Yeah," he said. "I've got the letter here that your grand-mother left for you. No, I haven't a clue what's in it. It is something that goes above and beyond her will, in which you figure prominently, as you learned a short time ago."

"I wasn't sure," whispered Janice. Tears formed in her eyes and Chris took her hand.

"How did you find out about the will?" Tony asked. "Nobody knew how to get hold of you for a while, I know."

"I'm sorry," she said. "I was scared."

"Of whom?"

"Well, my first husband, for one," she said. "Then there've been a few other men who I thought might be trying to intimidate me. A guy at the Gas Station, for example, in Chapel Hill."

"Oh, yeah, I know who you mean," nodded Tony. "I'd forgotten. Word got around that you'd handled him in a fight and he wanted revenge, or getting even, or something."

"He attacked me when I worked at Gus' station," she said.

"I remember," he said. "I went to high school with him. Fortunately, I haven't seen him for a while, but he's always been a bully and no damn good, as I recall. In fact I remember hearing rumors that he'd sent some guys after you."

"They weren't rumors," she said.

"They weren't—you mean, he actually attacked you?"

"He certainly did," she said. "In fact, look, Tony, I'd appreciate it if you keep it quiet that we're around. I don't want to deal with some thugs that he's hired. We'll be gone as soon as I can get this inheritance stuff straightened out."

"Okay, I get it," said Tony. "You want me to list the house?"

"Yes, please," she said.

"Okay, I'll get the papers organized tonight and meet you with them tomorrow," he agreed.

"That's great," she said, and they shook hands.

"Now, what about the other place?"

Janice tried to answer, couldn't, and cleared her throat. Again, she couldn't quite speak.

"Honey?" asked Chris. "Something wrong?"

Janice managed to nod. "What other place?"

"The place in the Woods," Tony smiled. "Your grandparents owned it. I mean, your dad's parents."

Again, Janice couldn't speak. "You know about the place, don't you?" Tony asked. Janice shook her head. "It isn't too far from Wake Forest. It's pretty near the Falls Lake State Park."

"Falls Lake Recreation area?" said Chris. Tony turned to him.

"Yeah," he said. "The Falls Lake Park contains Falls Lake and more than 25,000 acres of woods. Your place can't be too far from there. I've never been there, but I've heard it's beautiful."

"It is?" asked Janice.

"Oh yeah," Tony said. "You got time to run up there?"

"This place is mine?" Janice had to whisper.

"Yeah," said Tony. "I've got the key and the address and some pictures. You go up to Purlear, as I recall."

"I think I'd better get this other stuff settled first," she said. "Then we'll work out the other place." Her mind was whirling with this new information.

"Jeez," said Chris. "You're tuning out to be a real estate magnet."

Tony snickered and Janice said, "That's 'magnate'."

Tony departed and Janice and Chris talked. "Well, a nice house sounds pretty good, Jan."

"I agree," she said. "Look: we've got to get rid of this creep who's been stalking me. Then we'll worry about the inheritance."

"Okay," he agreed.

*****

The Great Father told the commissioners that all the Indians had rights in the Black Hills and that whatever conclusion the Indians should come to and be respected. I am an Indian and am looked on by the whites as a foolish man, but it must be because I follow the advice of the white man.

Chief Shunka Witko (Fool Dog.) Brown, p. 274.

CHAPTER TWENTY-SIX

Janice directed Chris out of town and to Plum Point, located on the Pamlico Sound. "My cousin and the man who would become her husband found Blackbeard's treasure out there," she told him, pointing to a small island in the Sound. "It's called St. Margaret's Island."

"Wow," he said. "Hasn't that treasure been there for three centuries?"

"No," she said. "It was originally buried on Plum Point, but Anna's grandfather found it and hid it on St. Margaret's."

They stopped at the Pamlico Inn Bed and Breakfast, and the owners came out and greeted them warmly. "Haven't seen you for years, Janice," said Greg, who had gone to high school with her. "Heard you got your degree, all that, huh?"

"Yeah, she did," said Chris. "And she's going to finish work on a doctorate real soon. We want to do a little honeymoon here, since we were just married."

The owners congratulated them and showed them to their bridal suite, where Janice spread the materials on a table near the window.

"Er," said Chris.

"Yes?" she said.

"Well, I was just thinking that, you know, we should…er…try out the bed and make sure it's okay, you know?"

So, the material didn't really get considered for some time that afternoon. Still, both agreed that the interlude was well spent and the bed more than satisfactory, to say the least. That evening, they adjourned to the Outer Banks for dinner.

Janice selected a supper club called Pamlico Jack's Pirate Hideaway that served seafood. Again, the seafood astounded Chris, and Janice, who had grown up with it, loved showing her husband the outstanding cuisine offered by her hometown. Chris ordered crab cakes and pronounced the North Carolina delicacy delicious.

They ordered coffee and relaxed for a few moments. "What do you think?" she asked.

"Do you know a lawyer in town?" he asked. "I mean, I'm sure your buddy is good, but we need someone to advise us on estates."

"Someone who specializes in wills and investments," she added.

"Can you find someone like that or should we take the stuff back to Oklahoma?" he asked.

"I think that if we do it here we can make it a lot more convenient, don't you?"

"Yeah," he said. "We just have to have a way to access the money if you want to use it."

"Not a money market, right?"

"I wouldn't think so, at least for a long-range thing."

Janice frowned. "Perhaps we can establish a link from a Raleigh bank and an Enid bank." He agreed.

"I suppose they can advise us on security, too." They finished a piece of pecan pie, made with local pecans. Again, Chris told her that the pie was so good that his knees had gone weak.

"Are you really trying to fatten me up?" he teased.

Back to the bed and breakfast, and they fell asleep in the soft, comfortable bed. Breakfast included an unusual egg, cheese and sausage casserole, and they obtained several decorating ideas from their hosts.

Janice stared in open admiration at the kitchen cabinets. "These are just beautiful," she observed.

"The secret is automotive paint," said Greg. "A friend of mine owns an Auto Body Shop. Well, he owed me a favor, so I took the cabinets to him. He sprayed them with automotive paint and baked them in his shop lights."

"I have to remember that," said Janice.

"None of my business, Janice," said Marcia, the owner. "But are you going to visit your house in town?"

Janice smiled, and then explained that she just learned she owned a house in the forest near Falls Lake. Marcia and Gregg exchanged glances.

"Do you know the place?" asked Chris.

"Not exactly," said Greg. "I've heard the stories, however."

"What stories?" asked Janice, surprised.

Greg set down a plate full of homemade pecan rolls that Marcia had baked that morning.

"Now, dammit, Greg, do you have to tell your stories?" smiled Marcia.

"Maybe you're right," Greg hesitated. "No sense in putting these guys off."

"Oh, for heaven's sake," complained Chris. "Tell us."

Both Greg and Marcia chuckled. "Nothing, nothing," said Marcia, serving several more rashers of bacon. "Only superstitious rumors, that's all."

"Well, anyway, I think we'll probably put that place up for sale, also," said Chris, with a glance at Janice who agreed. "We both think that our lives are going to be located in Oklahoma from now on."

"As I recall, you don't have a lot of great memories of this place, do you, Janice?" asked Marcia.

"No," said Janice. "No, I certainly don't. I feel like I never fit in here."

"Are you going to see your grandparents when you get up to the woods?"

"Sounds like a good idea. This would be your mom's parents, right?" asked Chris.

"For sure. I haven't seen them in a long time and need to talk to them. Besides, you need to meet Grammy and Grampa," Janice said, looking at Chris.

Janice became quiet and then said, "I didn't really know my Dad's parents as well as I would have liked. I only saw them a few times a year, to my regret, so I was really surprised to learn I was the heir to their estate."

"What happened?" asked Chris.

"I don't know," said Janice. "I know there was some sort of falling out—"

"Oh, yeah, I remember," said her friend Marcia.

An awkward pause ensued, during which all three of the other people stared at Marcia.

"Well?" said Janice. "Tell me, for heaven sakes."

"Okay," said Marcia. "Your grandmother felt that her son was marrying Indian trash for some unknown reason. Even though your mother was beautiful, your grandmother didn't feel she was worthy of her son. It also caused a rift between both sets of grandparents."

"I think your dad came to resent the rejection of his wife by his parents," said Greg. "He cut off all communication with his parents for awhile but there was eventually some reconciliation about the time you were born."

"What else can you remember?" asked Chris. "You know Janice has had many threats and been stalked over the last months."

"My gosh, Janice," said Marcia. "That's terrible. Why would anyone in the family be angry with Janice. I certainly can't imagine it has anything to do with an old family feud."

Greg added, "You know a lot of people believe that your mother's family, Janice, still has some sort of secret that they've hidden for years, and that they have a secret fortune."

"Really?" asked Janice.

Greg nodded. "The people in your family have always believed you need to carve out your own way, I know that. You don't remember your dad's mother well, but she paid most of the expenses on your parents' funerals."

All this new information stunned Janice. After another fine dinner that evening in the Outer Banks they returned to their room at the bed-and-breakfast and changed for the night.

"Well, what do you think?" asked Chris as they climbed into the bed.

"I don't know what to say," said Janice. "I truly had no idea that my heritage involved some intrigue."

"Talk about a gift for understatement," he chuckled. "We seem to be in the middle of some ridiculous, antique family mystery that might be endangering our lives."

"What should we do?" asked Janice, puzzled.

"I'm not sure," said Chris. "I guess we have to let things play out for awhile. Remember, they put those bugs in your luggage?"

"Yeah," she said. "But we found the little things and they haven't been able to track us for a while now, right?"

"I hope so," he said.

*****

I never want to leave this country; all my relatives are lying here in the ground, and when I fall to pieces I am going to fall to pieces here (The Black Hills.)

--Shunkaha Napin (Wolf Necklace.) Brown, p. 274.

CHAPTER TWENTY-SEVEN

Since Janice hadn't been to her Grandparent's house for several years, she was excited to see them again. They settled their bill at the Bed and Breakfast and arranged to leave early in the morning.

Their hosts had set out warm, homemade cinnamon rolls, coffee and juice in the morning, and by 7:00 they were on their way. The route was a little confusing, as usual, and they made a couple of wrong turns, but by the early afternoon they arrived at a large, beautiful house nestled into the North Carolina woods at the end of a long, private road.

Chris, who'd taken a turn at the wheel, sat in some amazement as the house appeared at the end of the driveway. "Yow," he said at last.

Janice raised an eyebrow. "Did you say, "yow?"

"That's a gorgeous home," he said. "And this will be yours someday as well?"

"It sure is beautiful, " said Janice. "And yes, someday it'll be ours. I don't think I mentioned that Grammy and Grandpa are pretty wealthy."

"So, I see," murmured Chris. He pulled the car in next to a garage. They climbed out of the car and walked to the door up a long winding path with immaculate landscaping, and a creek that wound back and forth under rustic bridges.

The door opened as they approached. "Grammy," cried Janice. She ran to a tall, elegant woman with long gray hair. The woman was dressed in buckskin with beaded moccasins and turquoise jewelry—beads, earrings, and a couple of large and beautiful rings. The resemblance between the woman and her granddaughter surprised Chris and made him smile.

"Little Shining Star," beamed the woman in greeting. "It has been far too long."

The two women embraced. Their affection radiated from the hug.

"This is Christopher, of course," said the woman.

"Yes," grinned Chris, seeing tears in the eyes of his wife and his grandmother-in-law. He came forward into a warm and gentle hug.

"Star called us when you got married. We were delighted and we are thrilled that you've come to see us."

"Thank you," said Chris. "Please, I don't know your name."

"My name is Sandra White Deer," said the woman. "As my granddaughter's husband, you, however, can also call me Gram, if you wish."

Chris handed his wife his handkerchief, and she used it to wipe her eyes. "Thank you," Chris said. "I am honored."

"My husband will be along in a moment," Gram smiled. "He's doing some devotionals in the woods. He will be pleased to meet you."

Gram turned and led them into the house. Another man, a servant with long black hair, shook hands with Chris.

When they sat together in the spacious living room, Gram took hold of Janice's hands. She told her to relax and be at peace. "Stay and rest, restore your life." she said.

"I have to fly, Grammy," said Janice.

"Will you then be able to stay?" Gram asked.

"We certainly don't wish to disrupt your life," said Chris.

"This house has been empty for too long," replied Gram.

"And I can see that you two need some rest. Stay with us for a few days and gain some perspective. Do you know Robert Frost?"

"Yes," said Chris. He shut his eyes and began to recite:

"Whose woods these are I think I know
His house is in the village, though.
He will not see me stopping here
To watch his woods fill up with snow.

My little horse must think it queer
To stop without a farmhouse near
Between the woods and frozen lake
The darkest evening of the year.

He gives his harness bells a shake
To ask if there is some mistake.
The only other sound's the sweep
Of easy wind and downy flake.

The woods are lovely, dark and deep,
But I have promises to keep,
And miles to go before I sleep,
And miles to go before I sleep."

"The woods are lovely, dark and deep," repeated Janice.

"They are, yes," said Gram. "But you can rest all you need to in order to keep your promises."

"Very well," smiled Chris. "And thank you, Gram."

****

The Indians consider the Land known as the Black Hills as the center of their land. The ten nations of the Sioux are looking toward that as the center of their land.

--Tahoka Inane (Running Antelope) Brown, p. 275

CHAPTER TWENTY-EIGHT

Janice took Chris' arm and led him into a homey living room, with cedar paneling and cherry wood furniture. "The craftsmen of the tribe made them," she whispered. "They are very comfortable furnishings."

"It's beautiful," he whispered back.

"Our room is up there," she said, pointing to a balcony at the west side of the great room. "The washroom is located next to our room."

They went upstairs and put their luggage into a spacious, paneled bedroom. "Let's wait to unpack," said Janice.

"Sure," he said. "I'd like to get to know your grandparents."

"Yes," she said. "They're looking forward to spending time with you, too."

They found Janice's grandparents sitting on a porch at the rear of the house. The porch was enclosed with screens and yielded a panoramic view of the estate. Grandpa offered them each a glass of lemonade.

"How far does your property extend?" asked Chris.

"About five miles south," said Grandpa. "It's pretty big. It's been in our family since well before the Civil War."

"Several of our ancestors are buried here on the property," said Grandma. "The family cemetery is a half mile or so that way," she said, pointing west.

"I'd like to be buried here also," mentioned Janice.

"I can see why you all love this place," said Chris. "It is so quiet and serene. But why wasn't it overrun during the Civil War? I would have thought this property would have been a key plum for an invading army."

The grandparents exchanged glances. Grandma shook her head a little, as if to say, "Don't say anything yet."

"We do have a pretty defensible property," said Janice. "You'll probably see what I mean while we're here."

"Huh?" said Chris.

"Yes," smiled Grandma.

"Yes, indeed," emphasized Grandfather.

"What do you mean?" asked Chris. Again, the family exchanged glances.

"Not now, okay?" said Janice. "But let me say that we're completely safe here."

Chris tried to pursue the matter a bit longer. He couldn't shake the curiosity that he felt about the enigmatic comments of the family.

"Janice," said her grandfather. "Are you concerned about your safety?"

"Perhaps a little, Grandpa," Janice returned. "Not while we're here, of course. I think we've kind of confused Chris, though."

The family tried their best to re-assure Chris. He smiled and became jovial, but he found himself puzzled that Janice seemed to be on edge.

After dinner and some visiting, Janice announced that she was retiring. Chris excused himself also.

Once they were in their bedroom, he changed into pajamas. He climbed into the king-sized bed and found his wife naked, to his intense pleasure.

After a delightful half-hour, he sat up in the bed and asked her, "Can we talk?"

She sighed. "I hoped you might forget it," she said. "I know how curious you are by nature. I guess we need to talk about it."

"This all just sounds so mysterious. What is going on? Why do you feel so safe here?"

She hesitated. After a few moments, she said, "Do you know about any of the legends of the Carolinas?"

He hesitated. "Well, I know that Britain used some of the colonies for their prison camps, rather than executing all the people they sent here."

"That's it exactly," said Janice. "When their sentence ended, the Crown assumed that they would return to Britain. A fair number of the prisoners, however, decided to forgo a return to their homeland. Some of them were captured, but not by any means all of them."

"These were still criminals, right?"

"Yes," she said. "Britain wasn't thrilled about them coming back, and several of those people wound up doing things that earned them a hanging or another imprisonment, this time at Marshallsea or the ghastly prison called Newgate. A lot of criminals didn't get out of those places alive."

"Yeah."

"But a few of them made their way into the interior of America. These became some of America's early settlers."

"Not the most desirable, either, huh?"

"To say the least," Janice agreed.

"Where are you going with this?" he asked.

"Well, you remember reading about the Salem Witch Trials, right?" Janice said.

"Sure," said Chris. She sat looking at him for a few moments.

Then he got it. "Were some of the people sent here imprisoned because of witchcraft?"

"You've guessed it," she said. "And I don't think the Crown really went out looking for them, either. It isn't like they wanted them back, so probably not a lot of effort was really expended."

"Do you mean they came here?"

"That's the theory," nodded Janice. "If they did, they formed a colony, and hid back in the woods."

"Near here?"

"That's always been the Tradition. Not many people go looking for them. They're pretty scary, as you can imagine."

"Gack," he agreed. "Are they really dangerous?"

"I don't know," she admitted. "I've stayed as far away from them as I can."

"What do you know about them?" he asked, after a pause.

"I think I've always been creeped out by the study of the Occult," she said. "They were pretty famous for trying to bend the Will of God."

"You mean Magic," said Chris.

"Yes, I do."

"I don't approve either," he said, comforting her.

"Something about these Carolina backwoods," she said. "I never liked to be too far away from our house and property at night."

"You're kidding," he snickered. "What could possibly frighten you about impenetrable darkness, assorted animal cries, and a bunch of psychotic loonies running around?"

"I guess it's nothing," she laughed.

"Nothing but that wild series of stories of people vanishing into the night, never to be seen again, I suppose you mean?"

But she didn't seem to be amused. Indeed, her look seemed to indicate that perhaps he wasn't so far from the truth.

****

About three hundred Oglalas (Sioux) who had come in from the Powder River country trotted their ponies down a slope, occasionally firing off rifles. Some were chanting a song in Sioux: The Black Hills is my land and I love it and Whoever Interferes will hear this gun.

Brown, p. 283.

CHAPTER TWENTY-NINE

They entered the gracious living room, where Grandma offered them some iced tea. Chris didn't ask, but he felt somehow that these people didn't have cocktails in the afternoon. Or in the evening. Or after dinner.

He asked Janice quietly. "No," she said. "Native Americans don't really drink, if they're wise. I might have a cocktail before dinner but never here. I've never seen my grandparents drink."

The conversation was relaxed and cordial. However, about five o'clock, one of the Native American staff came into the room. Grandfather excused himself and left the room with the man. He returned a few moments later, looking somewhat troubled.

"Any problem?" asked Grandmother.

Grandfather shook his head, but paused for a second or two before answering. At last he looked at his granddaughter. "Five men," he said. Janice looked surprised, and then troubled.

"What's wrong?" asked Chris.

"Nothing's wrong," she said. "We're safe now, at least for the moment."

"Are you going to stay for a while, then?" asked Grandmother, her voice registering concern.

"Perhaps we'd be wise to do so," said Janice, frowning.

Chris spoke up. "Are you saying we could be in danger if we don't stay here? If we leave?"

Janice didn't say anything. A moment or two passed. "Well, I've got to leave for a while tomorrow," she said. "I have an early flight. I'll be back in the early evening. Can you stay here without me?"

Chris stammered. "Well, sure," he said, and turned to Grandmother and Grandfather. "As long as you don't feel you have to entertain me somehow. There's a lot to do here."

The older couple smiled. "I'm glad you see it that way," said Grandfather. "Star will be safe, I can promise you."

Dinner was by no means ostentatious, but delicious, exceptionally well prepared, and served beautifully. The meal consisted of native Cherokee delicacies: fried squash bread, Tsalagi Stew, and baked cucumbers. Dessert included grape dumplings and Red sassafras tea. Fresh fruit and a few cheeses finished the meal.

Chris and Janice went to bed early, and talked for quite a while about the day and what had transpired.

"Janice," he said, "Are you sure you'll be okay tomorrow?"

"Oh yes," she said. "I'm a bit concerned about you, though."

"Why?"

"Well, things aren't quite the way they seem here, you know."

"What do you mean?"

"You haven't asked any more questions about my parents, or my other grandparents either, you notice."

Chris was silent for a moment. "Should I?"

Now Janice fell silent. A moment or two passed, and the silence was palpable.

"Chris, do you believe that I love you?"

"Of course," he said. "You've showed me more affection and love in the last few days than I have ever felt anywhere, at any time in my life."

"I know," said Janice. "It's because, for the first time in my life, I really love someone. There have been others, Chris. I've been with other men…"

"That's not a secret," he said. "I've known about it for some time."

"Yes, I'm sure," she nodded.

"But it doesn't matter to me," he asserted.

"It doesn't?" she returned.

"Of course not," he snapped. "What matters is who you are now, and how you feel about me now."

"You wouldn't have been allowed in here if we hadn't actually been married," she murmured.

"What?" he managed.

"I mean, these people know a lot about me," she smiled. "They would not have condoned, much less welcomed us, without a solid, loving marriage being evident."

"And they could see that we love one another," Chris agreed.

"Okay, yeah," she said. "But you don't quite understand. They are quite intuitive, more than I am. If they had sensed any hesitation on your part, they would have…well, let's say they wouldn't have welcomed you."

"I get it," he said.

"Look," she said. "It is absolutely vital that you not try to leave here without me. Stay in the house, or don't go anywhere without Gram and Papa. I want you to promise me."

"Are you kidding?" he asked, a bit incredulous.

"No, not at all," she said.

He hesitated. Then, "Is there a time at which this will become clear?"

She shook her head. "Just be patient, Chris, please."

He considered for a few moments. "Are the Cherokees famous for sorcery?"

"Huh?" she said.

"Consider the evidence," he said. "Your grandparents live in a beautiful home on what was originally part of Cherokee territory, but hasn't been for—what—two hundred years?"

"Well, yes, like that, I guess," she admitted. "A long time, anyhow."

"And this estate was not over run in the Civil War or any other conflicts?"

"Principally, the Civil War, that's right," she agreed.

"Janice," he said. "Can your grandparents actually hide this estate?"

"Go to sleep," she smiled. "Everything is okay, now."

*****

Crazy Horse had known that the world men lived was only a shadow of the real world. To get in to the real world, he had to dream and when he was in the real world everything seemed to float or dance, and this was why he called himself Crazy Horse. He learned that if he dreamed himself into the real world before going into a fight, he could endure everything. Brown, p. 289

CHAPTER THIRTY

Janice slipped out of bed seven hours later. She took her uniform and other garments, which she had laid out the previous evening. She showered and then dressed in the quiet room with the help of a night-light. Then she left the room, being as still as she could. Chris didn't budge. Still sound asleep.

She went downstairs, where she found the Cherokee servant Chinch waiting for her. Within ten minutes, the small private plane was in the air to Raleigh Durham. Janice joined her flight crew in Atlanta and flew to Chicago. She made a jump to New York, a four-hour jaunt to Los Angeles, back to New York, then back to Atlanta and Raleigh. In all, about twelve tedious hours, but worth it, she thought.

The driver pulled into the driveway to the big house. Janice, not to her surprise, saw things resolving themselves into recognizable shapes. Soon, she saw the driveway to the house appear, and the driver followed it to the house.

The house was fully visible, with outside lighting appearing to illuminate every square inch of the exterior. Microwave sensors were located throughout the property, and Janice felt confident that any movement outside, even a deer or a rabbit, could set off the sensors.

A guard stood in a booth at the end of the driveway. When the limo pulled up to the booth, he came out, checked identification with intense care, and waved them through.

Chris stood by the front door, clearly glad to see her. They embraced and he gave her a passionate kiss, and murmured a well-received suggestion about how they could redeem the hour or so between her arrival and dinner with her family.

The Carolina night was perfect: warm, clear, although with an excess of humidity to be sure, and many lightning bugs blinking on the lawn which stretched away to the wood line. What a lovely night, thought Janice, as she sipped her frozen lemonade.

"Good day of flying?" asked her Grandfather.

"As normal," she smiled. "No particular difficulties—" She paused, considering. "Well, there is something. Every once in a while, maybe a couple of times a month, a man shows up. He greets me like an old friend, and tells me he's glad to see me. He always wears a Braves hat—"

"A what?" asked Grammy.

"A baseball team based in Atlanta," said Chris. "They're one of the few teams in the south. Used to be, before the Florida teams came along—Miami, Tampa Bay—the Cardinals were the big team in the south and the west."

"People rooted for teams outside their own city?" Grandmother asked, sounding a bit surprised.

"Oh yes," said Chris. "Before the Dodgers and Giants moved to California, almost everyone west of the Mississippi River was a St. Louis Cardinal fan."

Grandpa shrugged. "Yes, I do remember that."

"Same with the Braves, for a while," said Chris. "In the south, I mean."

"Right," said Grandpa.

"Anyhow," said Chris, a little impatiently. "Janice, you were saying?"

"Sorry," she said. "This guy always looks familiar, like I know him. But I can't place who he is. And there's something else…"

"Well?" asked Chris.

"He vanishes from time to time," said Janice, aware that her hosts would more than likely think that she was crazy. "Sometimes he's there, sitting in a seat near the middle of the plane. He calls me over to talk to me, but when we land and begin to de-plane, I never see him exit."

"Do the other flight attendants see him?" asked Grandfather.

"They have a couple of times. Look, I know what you're thinking, and this isn't my imagination. Something is happening. Something is about to happen."

"Like what?" asked Chris.

"I'm going to get a bit esoteric, friends," said Janice. Grandmother and Grandfather sat and looked at her. She sat next to her husband and took his hand.

"Do you ever read the Bible, Grandmother and Grandpa?" she asked.

Gram and Papa glanced at one another and shrugged. Then they nodded their heads. "What about you, Chris?" she asked.

"You know I do," he frowned. "I'm even in a couple of studies at the church."

"Right," she said. "I'm sorry if I insulted you. But I do need to know where you stand."

"You saw my friendship with my Pastor, Janice," said Chris with a shake of his head, registering puzzlement.

"Well," she said. "Do you know what a Blood Moon is?"

"Sure," said Grandfather.

"It's what happens when the Moon turns a red color," said Gram. "Indians see them as messages from God. It's regarded as rare, I think."

"That's true," she said. "But when they appear, they are also interpreted by the faithful as communications from God."

"What do they mean by communications?" asked Gram.

"When they appear, they mean that something is about to change," said Janice.

The room became silent. The three-people looked at Janice and at each other. "What is going to change?" asked Chris.

"I can give you some examples," she said. "A pastor named John Hagee leads a mega church in San Antonio. He says that previous blood moon cycles coincided with major events in Jewish history: For example, in 1493, as Jews were expelled from Spain; in 1949, the state of Israel was founded; and in 1967l, Israel fought its Arab neighbors in what has been called the Six Day War."

"Oh," said Chris.

"Yeah," said Janice. "In other words, it does seem to mean that something significant is going to occur."

"Where did you learn this?" asked Grandmother.

Janice gave an informal bibliography of the literature she'd studied. Grandmother and Grandfather listened with interest.

"What do you think is about to happen?" asked Grandfather.

"It is difficult, even impossible to guess," admitted Janice. "I thought, for a while, that the earth might rebel against the evil that has been done to her."

"Evil?" said Chris.

"We are seeing the destruction of many of the things that give the planet life," Janice said. "I'm as guilty as anyone, of course. But on occasion someone says something that is obviously silly, but it is adopted and viewed as truth by people who don't live in the land or understand it or love it."

"What can we do?" asked Grandmother.

"Make people aware," said Grandfather. "There was an admirable campaign in the fifties here in America which advised people not to be 'a litterbug.'"

"I remember," said Grandmother. "People used to think nothing of throwing trash out the windows of their cars, assuming that someone would clean it up."

Janice nodded. "The campaign actually had some success," she said. "Maybe that's the answer. Rather than trying to solve every problem all at once, we pick one thing and work on it until things get better. Then we move on to something else."

"Come," said Grandmother. "Let us have our supper."

Chris realized how warm and comfortable he felt with Janice and her gracious relatives: so generous, so wise—yes, that was the right word. There. was a depth to these people. They had managed to put the concerns of the world behind them and focus on loving one another, the world, the woods, and even their backgrounds.

*****

The Cheyennes also distinguished themselves that day. Chief Comes-In-Sight was the bravest of all, but as he was swinging his horse about after a charge into the soldiers' flank the animal was shot down in front of a Bluecoat infantry line. Suddenly another horse and rider galloped out from the Cheyennes' position and swerved to shield Chief Comes-In-Sight from the soldiers' fire. In a moment Chief Comes-In-Sight was up behind the rider. The rescuer was his sister Buffalo-Calf-Road-Woman, who had come along to help with the horse herds.

--Brown, p. 290.

Chapter Thirty-One

Chris woke to find his wife dressed, standing over him. "What time is it?" he groaned.

"Late," she said. "I am pleased at how you are relaxing, Chris. You seem to be stepping into a new world."

"True," he said. "I'm feeling a great deal of peace."

"We'll try to set that as the way to lead our lives. Relax, enjoy the time we have."

Chris rose, showered and went down to breakfast. "Why don't you go up to the caves?" suggested Grandmother.

"I would like to," said Janice. She squeezed his free hand.

"Sure, let's go," Chris said.

At that moment a light started to flash above the door to the house. "Someone is on the property," said Grandfather. "Come, Janice, let us walk down there."

"More than one," said Grandmother. She was staring into the middle distance, at a spot on the door, where no one could see anything.

"How many?" asked Grandfather.

"Four, I think," said Grandmother. "They are armed, also."

"Do you think they have followed us here?" asked Chris in a whisper to Janice. She didn't respond. Her face was pale, now, and somewhat fearful.

"What's wrong?" Grandfather asked.

"They're killers for hire, Grandfather," she said. "They have come for me. I'm sure that they were hired to kill me by that man I told you about."

"How would you know..." began Chris, but then grew

silent, seeing that his wife was serious. She, like Grandmother, stood staring somewhere into the middle distance.

"Do you want me to handle it?" asked Grandfather.

Janice managed to nod. Grandfather picked up his telephone and touched a few numbers. "Four," he said into the mouthpiece. He gave the location. "Sit and relax, dear Janice."

Janice took a chair, her face ashen with apprehension. "Grandfather," she said. "Do you need my help? Because I'm quite willing…"

"No," said Grandfather. "Please do not worry. All will be all right."

Ten minutes passed. Chris continued to watch Grandmother and Janice, who had not ceased to look apprehensive.

Then, as if a switch had been thrown, Grandmother and Janice relaxed. "It's all right," said Grandmother. "They're no threat now."

"The men?" asked Chris. "Gone?"

"Not exactly," said Janice, who looked relieved.

The phone rang. "Yes?" said Grandfather into the phone. "Very good," he said. He turned to Janice. "Do you want to see them?"

"Perhaps it would be wise," said Grandmother.

"Okay," nodded Janice. She reached for Chris' hand and led him from the room. She took him out the front door, and then down the driveway.

Two men greeted her. "This way," they said, and pointed to the woods. To Chris' surprise, a path appeared and Janice led him about twenty-five yards down the path. They found themselves next to a small stone house, which seemed to be quite old.

A guard opened the door and Janice walked in, still holding Chris' hand. They found themselves in a large room, which appeared to be a great deal more spacious on the inside than it seemed from the outside.

At the far wall, Chris saw four men, gagged and bound hand and foot, leaning against the wall. "What shall we do?" asked the guard. "The cave?"

She shook her head. "No, I don't think so. Let's clear them and send them back home. They won't have any memory of this if we do it right."

The guards nodded. The captives didn't seem to welcome this news, but they seemed incapable of speech, though their eyes looked terrified.

Two guards pushed the men through the door at the far end of the room and pulled it shut behind them.

"What's in there?" asked Chris.

"Nothing," she said.

"Can I see?" he asked.

"Sure." She led him to the door and opened it. As she had said, he saw nothing except some swirling fog.

"Where are they?" he asked, staring in surprise. That the men would have vanished seemed impossible.

She smiled. "They're back in town. They have no memory of anything since they walked onto the property."

"But…" he stammered. "What on earth…"

The two men who had taken the captives through the door walked up and smiled at Janice. "Everything's okay now, Star," one of them said.

Janice thanked them and went back into the house, still holding Chris by the hand. She looked troubled.

"What are you still upset about, Honey?" asked Chris gently.

"I'm thinking they aren't going to stop coming after me, Chris," she said. "Their boss is intent on taking vengeance for the harm he thinks I did to him."

"Did you?" asked Chris. "Did you damage him, I mean?"

"Grandfather made some inquiries for me," she said. "He'll never be able to talk in a normal voice again."

"Do you feel responsible, or guilty about it?"

Janice bit her lip. She didn't answer for a moment. "I have never wanted to hurt anyone, Chris. I've made several bad decisions, I agree, but those were my fault."

"Look," he said. "That guy grabbed you and threatened you. He had no right whatever to put his hands on you. I'm talking about that incident at the gas station, you know, when you smacked him? The judge warned him and told him to stay away from you."

"It isn't a matter of legality," she explained. "Sure, the law is on my side. If he could have sued me and the station and the franchise company successfully, he thinks he would have made some money. Maybe a lot of it."

"Yeah, but he didn't, and he couldn't," said Chris.

"That's the point," she said. "The fact that he never could have won doesn't alter his conviction that he was in the right."

"I don't..."

"Look at it this way," she said. "A college friend of mine, Linda Norris, told me a couple of stories about her dad."

"Linda's dad?"

"Yeah," she nodded. "He was an insurance investigator for a major company. His job, specifically, was to investigate for fraud in claims."

They walked into the living room and were greeted by Grandmother and Grandfather. Janice told them that the situation had been dealt with and re-told the beginning of her insurance fraud story.

"So one day, Jack—that was his name—was assigned to adjust a claim from the West Coast. A guy went to his bank, borrowed a lot of money, and began to build his own sailboat. It was a real beauty. He took out a huge insurance policy on the boat as he finished it."

"Not tracking, Honey," began Chris.

"Just hang in there." She continued. "According to his claim, he set out from Los Angeles one night to sail down to San Diego, all by himself. The night was rainy and stormy, with higher than usual seas."

"This was an inexperienced sailor?" said Grandfather.

"Yes," replied Janice. "According to his report, he made it down to about LaJolla. Then, in a terrible accident, his boat hit a floating log, split at the front, and sank into the Pacific, about five miles from shore. Fortunately, he had a surfboard on the boat, and managed to row himself to shore on it. He came ashore at the home of a friend, who called the Coast Guard. They did a search, but saw no trace of the boat."

"No floating debris, life jackets, or anything?" asked Grandpa.

Janice shook her head. "Jack gets to Los Angeles, sees the pictures of the boat, the dock, all that. He's about to approve the claim, but he gets a call from the agent who'd sent it to him."

"She was suspicious, huh?" said Grandfather.

"Yes," said Janice. "Jack goes to see her, and asks why she didn't pay it."

"They didn't pay the claim?" asked Grandpa.

"The Agent, whose name was Charlene, tells him that she just couldn't do it, For one thing, this was a novice sailor, and he was going to sail from Los Angeles to San Diego on a night with high seas, stormy weather, rain, etc. She just felt the claim felt funny."

"It does, even to me," said Grandmother.

"Well, yeah," agreed Janice. "Jack went to Los Angeles, and to the harbor where the boat was docked. Yes, the owner had rented a slip for the season. When Jack went to the marina, though, he couldn't find anyone who remembered the boat. One guy said he remembered that the slip had been vacant for a whole season, and no, he didn't remember the boat."

"Uh, oh," grinned Chris. Janice went on.

"So they called the man in for a conference," she said. "After some intense questioning from the agent supervisor and the company lawyer, he admitted that there never was a boat by that name."

"How did they figure that out?"

"They learned that the owner purchased some plans, took out the loan and bought the wood, sails, fitting, etc. He took the receipts to the bank, and they approved the plans, and then he returned everything. A few months later he took a picture of another boat and brought it in."

"Brother," said Chris. "He thought no one would see through this?"

"Exactly," said Janice. "At the meeting, he confessed to everything and went to jail for fraud. The bank got most of their money back."

"A big problem with criminals," noted Grandfather. "One

characteristic is that they believe they are smarter than anyone else. So, this man thought he could get away with building a non-existent sail boat."

"So you're saying that this guy who's—er--stalking Janice—I guess that's the right word—thinks that he can out-think everyone involved in this?" said Chris. "Kill her? Harm her? Nobody will know he's involved, he's figured."

"He can think what he wants," said Grandfather. "He's not going to succeed, I guarantee it."

"Thank you, Grandfather," said Janice, just a bit above audible level.

"Come on," said Grandmother. "Let's go to the cave."

*****

The Whites told only one side. Told it to please themselves. Told much that is not true. Only his own best deeds, only the worst deeds of the Indians, has the white man told.

--Chief Yellow Wolf of the Nez Perces.

Brown, p. 316

CHAPTER THIRTY-TWO

Chris took his wife's hand and they followed Grandmother and Grandfather through the house. "Why are we going to the cave?" whispered Chris.

"Grandfather thinks we'll be safer there," she said. "As a matter of fact, I think you're going to love it there. It isn't what you expect."

"What do you think I'm expecting?" asked Chris.

"You're expecting rocks, and stalagmite and stalactites, with lots of hidden rooms, a gigantic main room, and torch light," she returned.

"Well, yeah," he said. "Sort of like Tom Sawyer with Injun Joe hiding out. Danger at every hand."

"Uh, huh," she said.

In a few moments they were walking through the woods and headed toward a mountain about ten miles away. "A long way," said Chris, not relishing a walk of several hours.

"Just a moment," she said. "Hold on."

Grandfather turned off the path in about 50 yards and walked a few steps into the woods. He drew aside a piece of undergrowth and the group saw a black opening. He smiled at Chris and motioned him forward.

Still holding his wife's hand, Chris walked into the blackness. He took a few uncertain steps in the pitch-dark and said, "Do you want to take the lead?"

"What's the matter?" said Janice. "Just keep walking. You'll be fine."

She stepped up next to him and put her arm around him. In two more steps, everything changed.

*****

I have asked some of the great white chiefs where they get their authority to say to the Indian that he shall stay in one place, while he sees white men going where they please. Let me be a free man—free to travel, free to stop, free to work, free to trade where I choose, free to follow the religions of my fathers, free to talk and act for myself—and I will obey every law or submit to the penalty.

--Chief Joseph of the Nez Perce. Brown, p. 330.

CHAPTER THIRTY-THREE

Chris blinked as a huge lighted cavern appeared a few moments later. He turned and looked, but saw nothing but a black corridor behind him. As his eyes adjusted, he realized that he had come into a large village. It was obviously well ventilated, for the air was clean and pure.

Somehow, the light was natural. It was bright enough that he could see doors on the sides of the large room, and a market in the middle.

"Janice," he said. "What is this?"

"This is the old way of Cherokee life," she informed him. "When the troops forced our people to evacuate the Carolinas, many of them left and walked all the way to the Oklahoma Reservation. Quite a few of those Cherokees died. However, a lot of people from our tribe stayed here and hid in this cave," Janice continued. "Others have come back and settled here again."

"Just your tribe?" he asked.

"No," she said. "We also brought in some of the Creek tribe, also the Seminoles, and the Choctaw."

"The tribes of the Southeast, in other words," added Grandfather.

"Is this area completely self-sufficient, then?" Chris wondered.

"We have doctors, a medical clinic, schools and other services," said Grandmother. "Our people go in and out to the nearby communities, of course, to buy clothing and hardware, for example."

"What about food?" Chris asked.

"We raise most of it in in fields near the cave," said Janice. "Once in a while we send out a hunting party for deer, or we may buy cattle and butcher them for a meat supply."

"Why are you showing me this?" he asked.

She paused. "Have you ever heard of a great war chief named Red Cloud?"

"Yes, I think so."

"He got tired of the continual fights with the white man," she said. "He's famous for a quote: 'The white man came to our lands. He made us many promises, but he kept only one. He said he would take our land, and he took it.'"

Chris was silent for a while.

"Why do your people choose to live here?" he asked.

"Because it is a remnant of who we are," said Janice. "Did you ever read Exodus by Leon Uris?"

"Sure," said Chris. "One of my favorite books."

"Well, that book sort of illustrates how we feel," she said. "When the white man took our lands, he exiled us to Oklahoma. He wanted us to farm. We of course were not farmers at that time and so the reservation was not a huge success. When we lived here in the past we fished, and hunted for our food, just as the Israelis are farmers."

"So, it was a matter of a square peg being forced into a round hole sort of thing," he said.

"We do raise a lot of food: vegetables and so on. But a great deal of our diet is wild game, domestic cattle and so on."

"How many of you live here?" he asked.

"Several hundred," she smiled. "Come and meet the elders."

Grandfather and Grandmother led them to a large assembly area, and Chris felt like he'd stepped back a thousand years. He was in the middle of a city, with many people and a great deal of activity.

People greeted Janice as she walked, and Chris could see that she was well liked and respected. Many tribesmen greeted Chris and expressed their pleasure with Janice's new husband.

"I'm kind of surprised," said Chris.

"At?" she asked.

"Well, that I've received a warm welcome from your tribe," said Chris. "I don't know much about my ancestry, but I doubt that I have much Cherokee blood."

She grinned. "You have me," she said.

"Didn't your ex-husband fit in?"

She hesitated. "He was more Irish than anything else. That's not a disqualifier, but he had some prejudice against the Cherokee. I could never bring him here. He couldn't get over a prejudice toward Indians and our ways."

"What about your children? Did they ever get to come here?" he asked.

"No," she said. "It was a taboo subject with my husband and I never insisted."

Chris gave her a sharp look. "May I know why?"

"I'm ashamed of how I didn't speak up for my Native American heritage and how I neglected my role as a mother since they were born."

"How do you mean?" asked Chris.

"I don't like telling this," she said, after considering an answer for a few moments. "I saw it early on. The girls became sullen, disrespectful, and unkind. But I now feel it was because of my disinterest and lack of involvement in their lives."

"But you were their mother," he said. "Could you not have

worked with them? Give them a sense of who they are, what their history is…"

"You have to remember," she said, "that at that time I was dealing with a failing marriage and a lack of self-respect, and so I never took time to instill faith or inspiration into their lives since it was lacking in mine."

"But…," Chris interrupted.

"Please, let me finish, Chris. Because of that their lives had little room for imagination and they lacked an ability to see the wonders, joy and beauty around them….as did I. To undo such a lifetime orientation is not easy. You are not that way, which is why I wanted to marry you. You and I will have remarkable children. They will embrace what is true, right and lovely."

"How can that be?" he asked.

"I think that my husband and I spent so much time arguing and fighting that we contributed to their attitudes, and also may have fostered it."

"Are you unhappy now?"

"Far from it," she smiled. "I've never been happier. I think because you love me and make me feel safe. Because I can count on you."

"I hear a 'but' coming on, though."

She nodded. "I still feel like I'm dodging my responsibility with my daughters."

"So…"

"One of the great poets said, 'Beauty is truth, truth beauty, – that is all ye know on earth, and all ye need to know.'"

"Right, Lord Byron, isn't it?" he said.

"John Keats," she corrected him. "Same era. But I think you remember that those two lines end the poem and they remain mysterious to most people."

"But not to you?"

"I know how I've always taken it," she said. "I never could get my daughters to go along with it. They saw truth as money, jewels, huge cars."

"And you don't, I take it."

"Not anymore," she asserted. "I know that your concern is for others and their welfare. You don't grasp, you give."

"So we see truth—"

"As beauty, yes," she agreed.

"What now?" he asked.

"I think we're going to use the tribe and end this," she said.

"You mean you're going to kill him?"

"I don't think we'll kill him," she said. "Nor will the tribe. No, I've got a plan. Grammy suggested it."

She went silent. He sat holding her hand for some time, watching her eyes. "Okay," he said.

"This is going to require your devotion and trust, though," she said.

"Of course," he said. "You don't really doubt me, do you?"

"No," she shook her head. "Again, if you had been dishonest or fickle, you never would have entered Grandpa's woods."

He nodded. "I think the word you're looking for is love," he said. She looked into his eyes.

"You mean you love me?"

"Can you believe anything else?"

"Not really," she said. "I sense your loyalty, your devotion. When you sat down on the beach with me at Rio, I had a sense at once at what kind of man you were. You are a person on whom I can build the rest of my life."

"I'm glad you feel that way," he said, trying to look serious. "It was easier for me, once I saw you in that Brazilian bikini."

She giggled and whacked his arm, though she was flattered.

"I don't want you harmed," she said, but choked a bit halfway through the sentence, and now the Cherokee discipline broke down. Tears ran down her cheek.

"Why would I be harmed?"

"Because I don't know what's going to happen to us," Janice said. "We may be fine. But I have to take care of this man who's harassing us.

"When you say 'take care' you mean…"

She grew quiet for a few moments. "I have a plan," she said. "Grammy is setting it up. Just trust me until I feel that we have to act. I think her idea is the best solution if the problem continues."

"Okay," he said without hesitation. "I don't want you hurt either."

"Then come on," she said, and took his hand. Two Cherokee braves came to stand with them in a few moments. They nodded to Janice and held out some clothing.

"Put these on," she said. He took the clothing and went into the bedroom and emerged about two minutes later. He was clad in supple buckskin, and soft but sturdy moccasins with intricate bead work on the top.

Then, Janice took the mug shot picture of the man whom she had hit in the throat and slipped it into a deerskin pouch bound around her waist.

Grandfather and Grandmother found Janice talking with Chris. "The elders want to talk to you, Janice," Grandfather said.

She followed Grandfather to a large arched doorway. Two

men pulled it open as Janice and Chris entered the room accompanied by Grandmother and Grandfather.

After some preliminary discussion, the tribal chief addressed Chris. "Your family," he said. "You will of course tell them about this camp. Will they be able to keep our secret?"

"Yes, they will," Chris said. "Indeed, with your permission, I would like for them to see this."

"Of course," said the Chief. "They might want to come and live with us as they grow older."

Chris realized how gracious this offer was, and couldn't form words to express his gratitude for several moments. He was overwhelmed with its generosity and managed to say so. The council nodded.

"We need to confer with you about this man who wishes to harm Star," said one of the men. "We don't wish to murder him. To do so is of course immoral, though he has scarcely behaved with grace toward Star. We would attempt to negotiate with him, but we do not have the sense that he would be responsive to any such approach."

"But even if we leave town," said Janice, "which we could do, he will track us down. He has been exceptionally resourceful in tracking us everywhere we go."

Janice mentioned where they had traveled, what towns they had visited, how they had varied their travel methods from airplanes to cars.

One of the men suggested that they return to Oklahoma. "How could we do that unobtrusively?" asked Chris. "I mean, would it be possible for us to leave here without leaving a track?"

"Oh yes," said the Chief. "We can get you home in moments."

"You can?" asked Chris.

Heads nodded all around the table. "Could we get back here as quickly?" asked Chris. "If we need to, I mean?"

"Yes," assured the Chief. "But again, I have to emphasize that this must be very secret."

Janice and Chris accepted the chief's offering to sleep in the compound that night before going back to Oklahoma. The servants at the home of Grandmother and Grandfather packed their belongings and brought it to them in their quarters at the Cave.

The dinner the group offered in the Cave that night was delicious, though not lavish. Grandfather explained that hunger had been a concern for years in tribal history, and talked about the 'Trail of Tears'.

"'Trail of Tears?'" asked Chris. "I don't quite remember the story."

"Yes," said Grandfather. He told the story of how the Che

Chris noticed that Janice's eyes had teared at the mention of the event. "It is an episode of sorrow, shame and even starvation."

"Many of us—not just Cherokees," said Janice, "but Creek, Choctaw and Seminole people as well—died."

"They just—stole your land, didn't they," mumbled Chris.

"Yes," said Grandmother. "They didn't take this compound and several other areas which we kept hidden from them."

"Kept hidden," repeated Chris. "How could you do that?"

"We have powerful medicine we can use when we need," said Grandfather. "It is not magic. You must know that our ancestors lived here for many centuries before the white man came. We could do things then—and many now—that they would exploit or misuse."

Chris and Janice embraced the elders and walked toward the archway that the Chief indicated. Janice embraced her husband's arm as they walked through.

They walked several steps in darkness but the floor was smooth and presented no obstacle. "Are you scared?" asked Janice, her voice comforting in the pitch black.

"We'll be clear in a few moments, right?" he said, trying to sound more confident than he felt.

He was correct. The light grew bright and they saw a couple of men standing ahead, holding their luggage and a tube, about five feet long, with a leather strap attached.

"What's in the tube?" he asked.

"You'll see," she said, slinging the tube's strap over her shoulder. "I hope I don't have to use it."

They stepped through a tall, oaken door which one the guards held open.

*****

"I have never heard Mr. Boone say he hated Indians," said Captain Russell.

"I'm sorry you don't hate them, Mr. Boone," said the Governor. "We are about to send an army against them. I had hoped you would enter it."

"I have never said I would not fight them, Governor, for I would. They must be conquered. They must be driven from the land."

"Aye!" said the others.

--Stevenson, Augusta. Daniel Boone: Boy Hunter. New York: Bobbs- Merrill Company, 1943.

The Childhood of Famous Americans Series. p. 183.

Chapter Thirty-Four

They had become used to North Carolina humidity and heat in the forest, but Enid, Oklahoma set a new standard for summertime heat. "At least it isn't raining," said Chris.

"Really," said Janice. "The humidity is so high that it might as well be."

"Well, you might as well get used to it if we are going to live here." A Native American man took their luggage and loaded it into the trunk of a cab. They climbed into the back and Chris gave the driver directions to their house.

"If we want to go back to Carolina do we come here?" asked Janice.

"We are available 24 hours a day, Shining Star," asserted the driver. "In the meantime, I have a phone number for both of you, that you can use day or night to get ahold of us. We can be here in moments."

"Thank you," she said.

"We consider you very special, Star," said the driver.

"I know all about that," agreed Chris.

"I appreciate that," Janice replied.

They arrived at his house and Chris had the driver stop down the street a block or so away.

"Do you see a car in front of the house again?" asked Janice.

Chris peered through the binoculars. "I can't tell," he said. "There are a couple of cars on the street. Let's go in the back way."

The driver went around the block and parked on the street behind Chris's house. He and Chris carried in the luggage, but

Janice took the cylindrical leather case. They went into the rear door of the house and down the stairs to the basement, where lights would not shine out.

"What's our plan?" asked Janice, after the cab driver had departed.

"We'll wait until it's dark," he said. "Then I go up and check. If someone's there, we'll deal with it. I'm hoping they don't know we're here."

She looked around the basement, and to her delight discovered that Chris had converted the area into a comfortable living space, with a well-decorated living room, modern kitchen with Jenn-Air appliances, and a washroom with a shower. "What do you want for dinner?" Chris asked.

"What are you offering?" she grinned.

"Well, how about a couple of martinis and appetizers to start, followed by a thick steak, baked potato and a salad?" She responded by starting to mix the drinks and a few moments later they were relaxing on the couch.

An hour or so later, Chris had her set the table while he prepared dinner in the basement's kitchen. Soon the delicious scent of the meal permeated the air.

The steak was perfect—charred black on the outside with a pink and juicy center. He produced a bacon and sour cream finish for the baked potatoes, and a homemade buttermilk ranch dressing for the salad. Chris opened a California Burgundy bottled by a fine central coast winery. He told her that it was his favorite winery and he purchased several cases per year.

"I'm sorry I don't have any tiramisu or baked Alaska for dessert," he teased. "Would a little fudge ripple ice cream suffice?"

Janice, not used to eating the way she had with her grandparents and Chris, shook her head. "I don't think I can manage to eat anything else, thanks. I didn't realize you were such a sensational cook, Chris. I think I may just put you in charge of the kitchen for us."

"I wasn't planning on a permanent job title." joked Chris.

They chatted for a few moments longer, but then Chris excused himself and went into one of the bedrooms. He emerged a few moments later wearing a black sweat suit, black shoes and a black watch cap.

"You stay here," he said. "I don't know how many are out there, and I don't want them to take you prisoner if these are the ones stalking you. Lock the doors behind me. I'll use my key to get back in. Do you promise?"

Janice shrugged. "I'll take that as 'yes'," he smiled. "All right, see you in a few moments."

He let himself out the back door and ran to the end of the block. Sure enough, two cars sat in front of the house, and two guys sat in each car. Moving silently, he approached the car in back and stuck an icepick into the two back tires. The men in the cars didn't react at first until they realized that the tires had gone flat. They jumped out of the car and found themselves staring at a Colt .45 and what looked like a ninja holding it. Less than a minute later, they found themselves lying flat on their faces, bound and gagged. Chris reached in the car and removed the keys and put them in his pocket.

The men in the front car had not reacted. Apparently, they were not being as attentive as they should have been. Chris fired a bullet into the lock on the trunk. The doors flew open.

The man behind the steering wheel fumbled with a shoulder

holster but Chris fired a bullet that grazed his shoulder and slammed into a large Crimson Maple on the other side of the car. He screamed in pain. The second man, stunned at first, jumped out of the passenger side and dropped to one knee. He raised his gun and began to say, "Hold it, Hero. Now put the gun down and ..."

He didn't finish the sentence. A yard-long arrow, fledged with gray goose feathers, slammed into his arm and pierced about half the length of the shaft, a razor-sharp head penetrating the car door, pinning him to the car. The man stood there, staring at the arrow. His scream pierced the Oklahoma night, but faded away as the shock of a desperate fear of the arrow and his wound overtook him.

Chris turned and saw his wife holding a Cherokee war bow, nocking another arrow. This arrow drove into the ground in front of one of the men lying on the ground and he screamed surrender.

He stared at her, taken somewhat aback at her skill. "So that's what you had in the leather case you brought along?"

"Yes," she said. "I'm delighted to see I can still shoot."

"Well," he muttered, "you certainly can, based on what you did here."

Janice took the pistols from the goons and stood guard over the men while Chris searched them. "No I. D.'s on any of them," he grunted as Janice completed a call to 911. Within three minutes four squad cars and an ambulance joined the cars parked on the street.

"Jeez," said the captain who commanded the response team after questioning Janice and Chris. "I'm very impressed, Mr. Hillman. We know a couple of these guys, some local talent thugs. What a couple of oafs. Strange, though. They've never done any muscle for hire stuff that we know of."

"Hmm," said Chris.

The police departed and Chris turned to his wife. "What now?" he asked. "I'm getting really tired of this nonsense with these hired mopes."

"Lock up the house," she said. "We have to go back to North Carolina now. We have to stop the person behind this."

"How can we do that?"

"We have to behead the snake," she said. "We're not going to stand for this anymore."

Within a few minutes they dialed their contact and were headed back to the portal.

Chapter Thirty-Five

They stepped through the portal into the cave and met a small group of Cherokee Braves waiting for them in the Carolina night. The Braves had a large conversion van and they drove off.

They turned onto a street in a pleasant neighborhood and stopped in front of a large house. Another entourage walked with surprising stealth through the streets. Another group followed them from the conversion van, which had been borrowed for the occasion from a family that was on vacation in Florida. The family was unaware of their complicity in what was about to happen, nor would they ever know what had transpired.

Gus, Janice's friend who owned the gas station, had given the group the address. He'd managed to find it using the Oil Company's database.

When they stepped into the driveway, Janice turned back to Chris and said, "Hold still."

She drew on his face with a warm red paint, then white, then blue. He said, "Can I please see a mirror?"

She worked at her own face paint, also smiling. "Perhaps in a few moments," she said. She didn't need a mirror, he noticed, realizing that she had done this before. In a few moments his wife had disappeared, replaced by a warrior princess. She drew back her long jet-black hair and secured it with a leather thong into a long fall behind her head.

She have a thumbs up to the two braves who left and ran behind the house, where they entered the back door with little difficulty. She nocked an arrow to her bowstring as they walked toward the house.

"Come," she said. Together they walked to the front door of the large house.

She removed a heavy war club from her belt and slammed it hard several times against the door. In a few moments, she did it again. This time they saw lights go on in your front room, and in a moment, the door opened. The man stood there wearing pajamas, a silk robe and leather slippers.

The man held a pistol, ready to fire at the intruders, but snarled in contempt, "What is this, Halloween?" Then he saw through the war paint. He recognized Janice and started to point the gun at her. "Say Goodnight, Pocahontas," he sneered with a bitter curse…

And screamed in terror as one of the Cherokee Braves fired a yard-long war arrow past his ear, which thudded into the wall behind him. The man noticed a warm stream running down his neck from his ear, which had been sliced by the arrow as it passed by. He felt a razor-sharp stone knife pressed against his throat. Another strong hand seized the pistol and pulled it upward. In his shock and terror, the man pulled the trigger and the pistol went off, the bullet flying up and away into the night. The braves yanked the pistol out of his hand in the next second. As Janice and Chris watched, the two warriors twisted his arms up behind his back. Then they lifted him a little and frog-marched him down the walkway to the waiting van.

The man was too stunned at first to respond. Then he gasped something unintelligible and opened his mouth to scream. Chris jammed a cloth into his mouth and the man struggled with a futile attempt to speak.

The front door of his house opened behind him and his wife appeared in the doorway. Stepping outside, she saw her husband being rushed down to the street. As she watched, not able to speak, two male Warriors lifted her husband and dumped him unceremoniously in the back seat of a dark, nondescript van, his hands and feet bound.

Two other warriors, one perhaps a woman carrying a long bow, climbed into the front seat and another behind the wheel of the van. With a gentle start the van drove off down the street, all lights off.

The kidnapped man's wife recovered enough to scream for help. Lights began to go on around the neighborhood and a few people came out onto their front porches, tying robes and rubbing sleep from their eyes.

The van would be found in the morning parked at its owner's home, in the garage, locked, secure and yielding no evidence in the kidnapping. The best efforts of the police could find no evidence pointing to the identity of the kidnappers: no fingerprints, no marks or any other physical evidence. Within a week, the investigation had reached a complete dead end. Of the woman's husband, the investigators found no trace and they never would.

CHAPTER THIRTY-SIX

"What is your name?" said a woman's voice.

The man, bound with his hands behind him in a chair, sat blindfolded, and found he was still gagged. As he struggled to spit it out, a hand seized his nose, and when he could hold his breath no longer, another hand yanked the cloth out of his mouth.

He gasped, making a struggle to get some words out, and found that a straw had been placed in his mouth. He sipped and some water gushed into his mouth. In a moment he gained the ability to frame a few words.

"My name is Simpkins," he said. "Who the hell wants to know?"

"You might want to lose the bluster, Simpkins," said another, masculine voice. "You are currently in a mortal situation, in case you hadn't figured that out."

Simpkins' mind was not functioning well. "*Where am I?*"

The woman's voice spoke again. "That isn't quite the right question, Mr. Simpkins. You'd be more correct to ask, '*when am I?*'"

"What does that mean?"

"You are in a cave in North Carolina," said the woman. "Again, though, the important thing is 'when'.

"Okay, when?" he snarled.

"This is the year 1506 A. D., and The Cherokee are the owners and occupants of the land." Simpkins cursed loudly and screamed for help.

"You don't seem to realize the danger you're in, Mr.

Simpkins," said the man. "You need to become a bit more-humble. We are many miles from any town or village so screaming will do you no good. You're in no position to make any demands or even requests."

The calm, quiet voices of the two-people had a chilling effect. Simpkins began to realize that he was in big trouble. "Okay," he said. "Am I being held for ransom?"

"No," said the woman. "The only ransom is a change in your approach to me."

"What do you want?" he asked, struggling not to shriek in his fury. The man had by now become aware that these people had him over a very large, uncomfortable barrel.

"Your attempts to murder me are what brought you here," said Janice. "I hope you will see this as a matter of self-defense."

"Yeah, **right**" sneered Simpkins.

Janice interrupted. "I have survived several of your attacks. We have just wounded a few more of your hired hoodlums. But if you ever try to attack me again you will find yourself here in the sixteenth century, rather badly unprepared to survive, for the rest of your life, which, I can assure you, will be far from pleasant."

Simpkins was gradually beginning to comprehend that these people had him at their mercy. "On the other hand," said the woman, her voice as cold as winter blizzard on the northern slope of the Bighorn Mountains, "if you agree to my terms, we will take you back to your century. You will be released several miles from here and will have to find your way home. Still, you will be safe."

"Okay, I'll stop," he said, his voice sullen.

"A bit more," said Janice. "I don't know how you found out

about the wealth of my family. However, I do know that whole charade is based on a desire to get your hands on my family fortune. You used the excuse of my punch in your throat to set this whole thing up."

They could see that Simpkins was amazed that the Indians had worked this out.

"I don't know what you're talking about—" he began to bluster.

"No, don't bother to deny what I'm saying," said the woman. "My investigators are very competent people. If the four men you sent to my grandparents' home had still had their memory, they could tell you that their lodge is exceptional in its security measures. The next men who come on to that property will vanish forever. The people you hired to harass us in Oklahoma are much the worse for wear. Now, if you agree to these terms, we will cut you free and blindfold you again. Then we will escort you back to your time and place."

A hand behind him yanked his hands upward, rough and painful. A knife cut away his bonds and yanked off his blindfold. Now another knife cut away the ropes on his legs and he blinked in the torchlight. He waited for his vision to clear, rubbing his wrists to start circulation in his hands and arms.

There. Under two torches he saw a couple of warriors— Indians with war paint—and he spied his chance.

He ran for the door. He yanked it open. He saw a forest outside and ran down a path. He heard a whizz sound next to his ear and saw an arrow slam into a tree ahead of him. "Stop," he heard the woman say. "Don't shoot, Firebird. He's made his choice. Let him go."

Then Simpkins left the illumination from the mouth of the

cave. He sped out into the night, running along a path in the woods. He chuckled to himself.

He'd shown them. All he had to do was follow the stars—

Except there were no stars, not tonight—

Nor a moon—

Near total darkness—

So, he didn't see the protruding tree root as he ran. He tripped, fell forward, and whacked his head hard on an oak sapling. He felt himself fading....

Then Simpkins found himself back in the chair, bound and unable to move, with Native Americans dressed in buckskin and wearing vivid and dramatic war paint standing all around him. His vision began to clear, and as it did, Simpkins became aware of another man, standing behind him. This man lifted Simpkins' wrist and using a sharp weapon, slashed the leather thongs that bound his wrists together. Someone removed his blindfold. Another man slashed at the bonds around his legs.

He looked around. He was in a cave illuminated with torchlight, with many warriors standing around him. As he watched, a half dozen men moved aside.

There. He saw the light. The opening to the cave. He sprinted past the braves and down the path.

He ran past a young tree and saw a body lying there. It looked like –

My god, it looks like me! Same pajamas, slippers--

He took his eyes off the path. An arrow flashed past his head and embedded itself in a tree. Distracted, he didn't see the root that loomed up and tripped him. He fell hard and fast, nor could he thrust his hands out to break his fall.

His head crashed with cruel, harsh force into young, sturdy

oak tree.

Then, with a startling jolt, he found himself sitting in the chair in a cave. His hands were tied. A knife. The cutting of the leather thongs. The run for the door. The escape. The arrow. The tree root.

Then, with a jolt…

Chapter Thirty-Seven

"Do you want to go back, Janice?" asked Chris. "Back home to Oklahoma, I mean?"

Janice nodded and took his arm at the elbow. The Braves took them back to the tribal cave and the transport. The four braves opened the door, and the group stepped through the time portal to their own time.

The married couple thanked the braves who had helped them, receiving nods of acknowledgment. Two women came forward and handed each of them a soft, exquisite, hand-woven, woolen blanket and the couple realized at once that the blankets would become heirlooms in their family. They thanked the women and the tribe and promised to return soon. Then the two of them stepped through the transport.

Enid, Oklahoma opened to Janice and her husband. No cars this time. Nothing but quiet. Nothing was stirring in the still of the night.

They stood in the street for a long time, two people who looked like Hollywood Indians in a John Wayne film. The night was pitch dark, and the husband and wife each had a Cherokee blanket wrapped around them. The blankets were soft, with Native American markings. The tribe had presented Shining Star with an heirloom wedding present.

"Are you ready to go, Star?" asked her husband, his voice gentle and kind. Her heart melted as she stepped forward and kissed him with all the emotion of the last few days caving in on her. She took his arm and led him into a grassy, beautiful knoll several yards from the road.

She leaned back. "Is anyone around?" she asked.

Chris looked at his watch. "No," he said. "No, it's the middle of the night."

She took his blanket and spread it on the ground. She peeled off the buckskin shirt and rolled it into a pillow. "Come on," she said.

In a few moments they lay in the warmth of the Oklahoma night, alone together on the blanket. She pulled her blanket over them.

At last they drew back, both relishing the delicious interlude under the stars of Oklahoma. They were two people alone in the world, as far as anyone else was concerned. "No mosquitoes," he noted with a grin. "This is perfect. Out of doors, free for good from the oaf who wanted to hurt us."

"Yes, perfect," she responded, her arms around him.

"You okay?" he asked, grinning in the dark.

"I feel wonderful," she said. "So that's the way sex is supposed to go. Delightful in every way."

"Remember what Woody Allen said after one of his sex scenes? 'That's the most fun I've ever had without laughing'." They chuckled and embraced a bit tighter for a few moments. "Well, I'll go a bit farther," he said. "That was the best time I've ever had at anything."

Janice gave a little laugh of agreement. "I know, and I agree about the sex," she said. "Still, I must say I regret the way things turned out."

"I suppose," he said, and they lay back together on the blanket.

"I wanted you to know," she told him. "I talked to Grandfather. I'm having him send some money to Simpkins' wife and kids."

"You are?"

"Yeah," she said. "I don't think they ought to be punished for his miserable decisions. Of course, Grandfather will make sure that they'll have no way of knowing or tracing where it came from."

"That's awfully nice of you," he said. "That's very generous."

"Some men, guys like Simpkins, have a hard time forgiving, don't they?" she asked, stroking his body.

"Yeah," he said. "C. S. Lewis once wrote that there is really only one sin."

His wife gave him a quizzical look. "I've read a lot of Lewis," she said. "I don't remember."

"It's the sin of Pride," he told her. "Consider John Milton's Paradise Lost, for example. Satan, according to Milton, rebelled against God, was badly defeated, given an opportunity to repent, but said 'Non Serviam' —

"'I won't serve,'" she translated.

"Right," he said. "So, he and his demons fell from heaven, and they fell, and fell, until they landed in what we call 'Hell.'"

"Yuck," she said with a shudder.

"Well, Satan chose not to think of it that way, remember?" said Chris. "On the contrary, he said, 'The mind is its own place and in itself can make a Heaven of Hell, a Hell of Heaven.'"

Janice nodded. "'Vanity of vanities, saith the Preacher, vanity of vanities; all is vanity,'" she quoted.

"Yeah," smiled Chris. "Biblical, right?"

"King Solomon, I think," she nodded. "Writing in the first chapter of Ecclesiastes."

"How'd you remember that?" he asked.

"Oh, when I was little, my grampa would make me memorize Bible verses if I misbehaved. I liked memorizing, so it wasn't really much of a punishment."

They chuckled together under the bright stars of an Oklahoma night.

"I had hoped Simpkins would see that he had to give up on this stupid mission to rub me out," she said. "Vanity, again."

"As you see," he said, "many people believe that acknowledging a personal sin or, as in the case of Simpkins, his bigotry and stupidity, is humiliating, diminishing, and means that people will think less of them." Janice agreed and they lay snuggled together for several moments.

With some difficulty, and unwilling to stop the embrace, Chris drew back a little. "Let me ask you something," he said. "How about if we rest up for a couple of days and then go to find your daughters?"

Janice's mouth fell open at this. In a few moments, she said, "Do you really mean it?" Tears clouded her deep brown eyes.

"Yes, I do," he said. "I talked to Grandmother and Grandfather about them when we returned to the house after Simpkins ran off."

"You did?" she said, a tear starting in her eye.

"Yeah," he said. "He said they'd be welcome in the compound. It sounds like they could use some of the tribal discipline."

"I guess that's true," she nodded.

"After all, they're half Cherokee. We could take them to the cave to live and work with the tribe for a year or so. I think that the Cherokee way of life could turn them around. I mean, if they had to work for their food, their clothing, all that, it might give them some hint of self-discipline."

"It had never occurred to me," said Janice. "That's a great idea."

"It isn't exactly mine," he confessed. "Remember a story from Sherlock Holmes, 'The Adventure of the Sussex Vampire'?"

"Sure, I loved the Holmes stories."

"Well, you remember Holmes' advice? 'I think a year at sea would be my prescription for Master Jacky.'"

"Oh, yeah," said Janice. "He was ten or thereabouts. Holmes felt that the discipline of a British ship of the line would probably do him good, right?"

"Correct," said Chris. "I think that learning in a new environment would probably help your daughters, don't you?"

"Not only that," Janice said. "Then I could use the transport to see them pretty often, and also keep track of them. Maybe it would help, huh?"

"I can't think of a better way of learning some life lessons," agreed her husband. "Anyhow, it would seem to be worth a try?"

They stood and dressed in the supple, comfortable buckskin. Then, they sat on the blanket again and turned to the East. The sun was just rising in a clear, lovely Oklahoma morning.

"That's our life, isn't it?" said Janice, smiling in the warmth of the Dawn.

"You bet it is," he said, kissing the top of her head. "Rising in the east, just like the sun."

"Very poetic, for a petroleum engineer."

He gave her a poke in the ribs and she laughed.

"Can we just rest in this warmth for a bit?" she said.

"Of course," smiled her husband, hugging her.

After donning their moccasins, they joined hands and walked without haste for a few miles until they came to their house. The warmth of the rising sun felt good against their faces.

*****

The Cherokee Braves returned to their century also, and a few of them went out a few weeks later. Outside the cave, they followed a path and came to a huge oak tree, which had been little more than a sapling in the century from which they had just stepped with Janice and Chris. Under the tree, they found a skeleton, remarkable because its skull had been smashed. It had been there for long time.

The Braves looked at one another and nodded. It looked like someone had bashed in the front of the skull.

*****

Today, the Cherokee Indians have a strong sense of pride in their heritage. The Cherokee rose is now the state flower of Georgia. Today, the largest population of Cherokee Indians live in the state of Oklahoma, where there are three federally recognized Cherokee communities.

CHEROKEE NATION
(AS PERFORMED BY PAUL REVERE AND THE RAIDERS.)

They took the whole Cherokee nation

Put us on this reservation

Took away our ways of life

The tomahawk and the bow and knife

Took away our native tongue

And taught their English to our young

And all the beads we made by hand

Are nowadays made in Japan

Cherokee people

Cherokee tribe

So proud to live

So proud to die

They took the whole Indian nation

Locked us on this reservation

Though I wear a shirt and tie

I'm still part red man deep inside

Cherokee people

Cherokee tribe

So proud to live

So proud to die

Songwriters

JOHN LOUDERMILK, JOHN D LOUDERMILK

Published by Lyrics © Sony/ATV Music Publishing LLC`

Read more: Paul Revere and The Raiders
- Indian Reservation Lyrics | MetroLyric

SELECTED BIBLIOGRAPHY

Brown, Dee. *Bury My Heart at Wounded Knee.* New York: Holt, Rinehart and Winston, 1970

"Cherokee". Wikipedia, the free encyclopedia. On-line, 2016

"Cherokee". On-line, Encyclopedia, 2016.

Cherokee. http://www.cherokee.org/, 2010.

Walt Disney, and Bill Walsh. Producers. Davy Crockett: King of the Wild Frontier. Norman Foster, Director. Walt Disney Films, 1955.

Hagee, John. Four Blood Moons. Brentwood, TN: Worthy Publications, 2013.

Loudermilk, John, and John D. Loudermilk. Cherokee Nation. Performed by Paul Revere and the Raiders. Published by Lyrics @ Sony/ATV Music Publishing, 1973.

North Carolina. Map of North Carolina. MapQuest Internet, 2016

Stevenson, Augusta, and Paul Laune, Illustrator. Daniel Boone: Boy Hunter. 1943: The Bobbs Merrill Company, New York.

Treuer, Anton. Atlas of the American Indians. National Geographic, 2010.

Viola, Herman. Indian Nations of North America. National Geographic, 2010.

Weisbart, David, Producer and Gordon Douglas, Director. The Charge at Feather River (1953) Warner Brothers.

Whitney, C. V., producer and John Ford, Director. The Searchers. Warner Bothers, 1956.

Ford, John, Producer and Director. Cheyenne Autumn. Warner Brothers, 1964.

Title: ACID

- Author: Jeff Lovell
- Publisher: TotalRecall Publications, Inc.
- HARD COVER ISBN: 978-1-59095-116-3
- PAPERBACK, ISBN: 978-1-59095-117-0
- EBOOK, Nook, Kindle, ISBN: 978-1-59095-118-7
- Number of pages: 352
- Publication Date: 2013

Rick Howell, living in the shadow of two women who have the power to change reality, must risk his life to stop the genocidal exploits of a desperate lunatic who wants to acquire their powers. The discovery of a mind controlling drug opens a pathway to frightening mental abilities for Rachel Farrell, who can move backward and forward in time at will, while Donna Riske, Rachel's best friend, can control the thoughts of others.

Title: The Coven of the Spring

- Author: Jeff Lovell
- Publisher: TotalRecall Publications, Inc.
- HARD COVER ISBN: 978-1-59095-113-2
- PAPERBACK, ISBN: 978-1-59095-114-9
- EBOOK, Nook, Kindle, ISBN: 978-1-59095-115-6
- Number of pages: 336
- Publication Date: 2013

An ancient secret, with frightening new powers, emerges to terrify and destroy.

Grace DeRosa, a gifted research chemist, lives with her husband Jim and their seventeen year old daughter Crissy. Grace finds a hidden spring in the woods near Salem, Massachusetts. She discovers that the consumed water imparts unique and fearful powers that lead to the ability to read minds, create terrifying mental pictures and force the user's will on others.

Title: Emerald

- Author: Jeff Lovell
- Publisher: TotalRecall Publications, Inc.
- HARD COVER ISBN: 9781590950807
- PAPERBACK, ISBN: 9781590950814
- EBOOK, ISBN: 9781590950821
- Number of pages: 348
- Publication Date: 2015

Emerald begins with a pirate assault on a merchant vessel. Blackbeard, or Edward Teach, terrorized the east coast of America from Nova Scotia down to the Virgin Islands. This book shows how people with a unique mental power called the Knack fight against the evil of pirates from 1715 to the present day, and even includes a long look at the court of King Arthur, and his chief advisor Myrthynne, who also had the most powerful manifestation of the Knack. This book, then, flows in several time periods and pulls together romance, villainy and a dramatic treasure, all of which frame a love story between a woman with the Knack and a man devoted to loving and protecting her.

Title: The Cape

- Author: Jeff Lovell
- Publisher: TotalRecall Publications, Inc.
- HARD COVER, ISBN: 9781590952078
- PAPERBACK, ISBN: 9781590952085
- EBOOK, ISBN: 9781590952092
- Number of pages: 228
- Publication Date: 2016

People say that *Der Fleigen Hollander — The Flying Dutchman*, as it is known in English — vanished with all hands in the sixteenth century off the Cape of Good Hope. Yet the ship has been by reliable, truthful people all over the world, suggesting that the ship is trapped in a time warp somewhere in the treacherous ocean south of the Cape. When her father is kidnapped by the ship, Therese goes to find him and rescue him from the self-imposed, Purgatorial imprisonment. In the search she is joined by her mother and a lifetime best friend, who seek to help Therese draw his soul back from the pit of Hell before he is lost for all eternity.

Title: The Ghost Of White Island

- Author: Jeff Lovell
- Publisher: TotalRecall Publications, Inc.
- HARD COVER ISBN: 9781590951194
- PAPERBACK, ISBN: 9781590952092
- EBOOK, Nook, Kindle, ISBN: 9781590952092
- Number of pages: 348
- Publication Date: 2015

In 1715, a ship's carpenter tried to rape the 14-year-old daughter of the captain of a British warship and was flogged almost to death. He mutinied and captured the ship, killing the captain and forcing his daughter into marriage. After falling in with Blackbeard, he abandoned his young wife on a cold, bitter rock called White Island, off the coast of New Hampshire. When he was caught and hanged by the British Navy, his treasure vanished into history. Many people believe that Martha, his reluctant wife, hid the treasure in the Isle of Shoals chain. This is the story of a search for those gold and jewels and treasure, protected by the Ghost of White Island.

Title: The Third Day

- Author: Jeff Lovell
- Publisher: TotalRecall Publications, Inc.
- HARD COVER ISBN: 9781590959947
- PAPERBACK, ISBN: 9781590959954
- EBOOK, Nook, Kindle, ISBN: 9781590959961
- Number of pages: 288
- Publication Date: 2016

The Old, old man walks in all the countries of the world, tracing and retracing and tracing again his betrayal, unable to find peace or grace since his betrayal of the Nazarene some two thousand years ago. Two newlywed young people and their spouses find themselves called to help him and recover an incalculably valuable treasure, worth far more than any earthly price. The group must go to the Virgin Islands and recover the treasure to help the Old Man redeem his soul and save others from a disastrous fate at the hands of a desperate cult.

Title: Jazz and Ella

- Author: Jeff & Jacqi Lovell
- Publisher: TotalRecall Publications, Inc.
- PAPERBACK, ISBN: 9781590953006
- EBOOK, ISBN: 9781590953013
- Number of pages: 104
- Publication Date: 2015

Jazz and Ella tells the story of Jazz, a fourteen-year-old high school freshman, and his best friend, Ella, who meet on the way to Disney World. A supernatural being gives them each a magic amulet, which the children use to transport themselves to new and different worlds. They meet and deal many situations that cause them to face their fears and even terrors; that suggest ways that situations can be handled; and they see some of the choices that they will have to confront as they grow up.

Title: Gina and Colby

- Author: Jeff & Jacqi Lovell
- Publisher: TotalRecall Publications, Inc.
- PAPERBACK, ISBN: 9781590953259
- EBOOK, ISBN: 9781590953266
- Number of pages: 136
- Publication Date: 2016

A Magic Amulet Allows Two Teen-Agers to Discover how to Make a Difference in the World of Animal Poaching Two teen-agers, different in every way, form an unshakeable friendship as a result of the adventures they share after meeting in Disney Springs. Transported through a magic amulet to a totally different culture and continent, they are offered an opportunity to make a difference in the lives of endangered animals.

Dangers abound as they face poachers and pirates in their attempts to rescue these creatures, and they discover a courage within themselves that leads each one to a positive change in how they view themselves and others.

Title: Marina and Dan

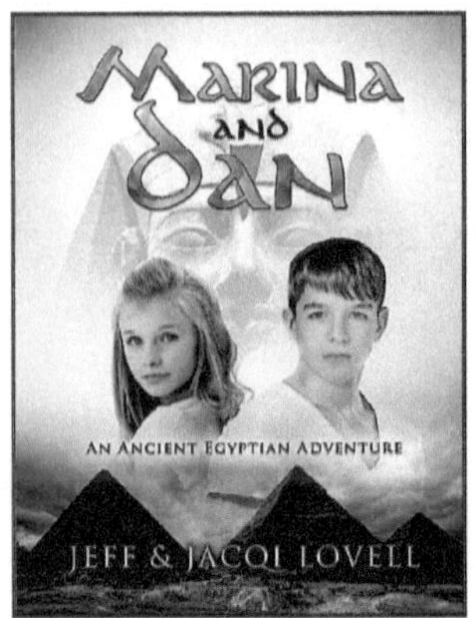

- Author: Jeff & JacqiLovell
- Publisher: TotalRecall Publications, Inc.
- PAPERBACK, ISBN: 978-1-59095-081-4
- EBOOK, Nook, Kindle, ISBN: 978-1-59095-082-1
- Number of pages: 128
- Publication Date: 2016

This ancient Egyptian Adventure, part of the Mouse Gate Series, traces the story of Marina and Dan, best friends since childhood, as they wrestle with the concept of heroism and how it applies to them. When offered a unique, but potentially dangerous opportunity by a spiritual being, they must make a decision that will stretch them in ways they never imagined. Able to experience first-hand the miraculous events that have been talked about for centuries, they witness the impossible become possible as they walk with Moses during the ancient biblical era where the crossing of the Red Sea took place. Both their friendship and their faith is strengthened through the adventures encountered together.

Title: *Max and McKenzie*

- Author: Jeff & Jacqi Lovell
- Publisher: TotalRecall Publications, Inc.
- PAPERBACK, ISBN: 9781590953334
- EBOOK, Nook, Kindle, ISBN: 9781590953341
- Number of pages: 150
- Publication Date: 2016

Max and McKenzie, teenaged twin brother and sister, receive magic amulets which allow them to time-travel to sites in ancient Israel. They witness Elijah's defeat of the prophets of Baal, and journey to the ancient temple of Solomon to assist in the removal of the temple treasures before the invasion of the forces of Egypt. They witness the theft of the Ark of the Covenant and its return to Israel by the Philistine forces, and march around the city of Jericho with the Israeli forces. In the climactic scene, they explore the Mount of Calvary to find the lost treasures of the temple. In their treasure hunting, they learn valuable lessons about self-confidence, personal faith, and persistent courage.

Title: The Captain's Daughter – A Macey And Luke Quest

- Author: Jeff & JacqiLovell
- Publisher: TotalRecall Publications, Inc.
- PAPERBACK, ISBN: 9781590957899
- EBOOK, Nook, Kindle, ISBN: 9781590957905
- Number of pages: 128
- Publication Date: 2018

Macey discovers her dad has taken a job across the country and must leave her home and friends. In order to soften the news, her parents take her on a vacation to Walt Disney World. At Blizzard Beach, she and a boy named Luke zoom down a water slide but pop up in water hundreds of miles away in the freezing Atlantic Ocean and a long way from shore. They are able to use a pendant that magically takes them to the shore of a secluded island. There a mysterious friend introduces them to the legend of the Ghost of White Island. The teens hear the courageous story of Martha Herring, forced into marriage with a brutal pirate, and abandoned on the miserable rock. The pirate goes back to sea, leaving Martha to guard his treasure. This is a recounting of her adventures and the challenges she and the people in her life endured. It is also the story of how the bonds of strong friendships can impact our lives.

Title: Cherokee Treasure

- Author: Jeff Lovell
- Publisher: TotalRecall Publications, Inc.
- PAPERBACK, ISBN: 9781590952344
- EBOOK, Nook, Kindle, ISBN: 9781590952351
- Number of pages:
- Publication Date: 2018

When I was a little boy, a great deal of television dealt with cowboys, and a great deal of that portrayed Indians as vicious killers. One movie had the lead character talking about the Oglala Sioux: "They're the throat cutters." But some of the most heroic and brilliant generals in our country's history were Native Americans: Crazy Horse, for example. Sitting Bull. Red Cloud, to name only a few. As a child, I was too young to have a sense of justice, I suppose, but I knew that it was wrong for the White Man to take the lands which were not theirs. It was wrong to slaughter the buffalo, as well, though the species seems to be making progress to repopulate now. Maybe I will succeed and give the land back to the Indians.